good intentions
agnès desarthe

translated from the French by Adriana Hunter

Flamingo

Flamingo
An imprint of HarperCollins*Publishers*
77–85 Fulham Palace Road,
Hammersmith, London W6 8JB

Flamingo is a registered trade mark of
HarperCollins*Publishers* Limited

www.**fire**and**water**.com

Published by Flamingo 2003
9 8 7 6 5 4 3 2 1

Previously published in English by Flamingo 2002
First published in France as *Les bonnes intentions* by Editions de L'Olivier 2000

Copyright © Agnès Desarthe 2000

English Translation copyright © Adriana Hunter 2001

Agnès Desarthe asserts the moral right to be identified as the author of this work
Adriana Hunter asserts the moral right to be identified as the translator of this
work

The publication of this book is supported by the Cultural Service of the French
embassy in London

institut français

ISBN 0 00 710095 7

Set in Minion by Rowland Phototypesetting Ltd, Bury St Edmunds, Suffolk

Printed and bound in Great Britain by Clays Ltd, St Ives plc

A catalogue record for this book is available from the British Library

good intentions

1

The Meeting

Becoming a home-owner is not without its disadvantages. There are the mortgage payments, the maintenance charges, the pre-War wiring, the hit-and-miss plumbing, the redecorating to do, and the total lack of sound-proofing in the walls and floors. Any notion of a carefree life stayed firmly out on the doormat. When we first arrived, I wondered whether I would ever shake my worries off again. It was not until the joint ownership meeting that I realised the full extent of the horror. These meetings were not compulsory, and it would seem an exaggeration to compare an optional form of torture such as this to the unavoidable concerns about paying bills and moving all our things. Where I am concerned this sort of logic does not, however, apply.

In response to the invitation from Monsieur Moldo, the manager of Gedeco, I find myself sitting in a small, overheated room listening to people talking for hours about things in which I couldn't be less interested, but on which I am nevertheless asked for my opinion and my approval. 'Let's vote on it, if you please.' Hands go up. Monsieur Moldo counts the votes.

'Madame Jauffret, are you sure you're against this?'

'Yes I am, absolutely.'

Madame Jauffret nods her head vigorously and then settles herself more firmly into her armchair to underline her determination.

'You do realise that each negative vote will cost the co-owners money?'

Did I hear that right? I dare not ask him to repeat it because I'm new and a little in awe of Monsieur Moldo. This is our 'uni', and I waste a fair amount of time wondering whether that is an abbreviation of 'union'. Monsieur Moldo looks like a tapir. The eyes are small, piercing and set close together; they manage to be mobile as well as slow, like minute surveillance cameras embedded on either side of his long pointed nose. Monsieur Moldo starts each of his sentences with 'listen', and you know straight away that you have lost. He never lets anyone interrupt him.

He welcomed us with open arms, Julien and me, crying: 'ah, new blood!', and I instantly imagined him chewing on my carotid artery. Behind him Madame Moldo, his wife, his double, his assistant, his secretary, a woman of many roles who wears her glasses low on her nose so that she can look over them, smiled at us, then took my hands and exclaimed: 'haven't you got beautiful eyes!' and then I remembered the brass plaque under the porch.

By the entrance there was a section of wall reserved exclusively for signs informing us that the building accommodated an ENT specialist, a dental hygienist, a psychiatrist, a graphic design company, our famous 'uni' and, finally, an 'Eye Bank'. No further information was offered. The black letters carved into the metal provided no complementary explanation. *Eye Bank – Second floor, right – ring twice.*

We were here, then, to give our blood and our eyes. I see.

I touched Julien's arm to reassure myself that I still knew the true texture of reality. Just touching the leather of his jacket, the suggestion of his skin and muscle beneath it, calmed me straight away. I gave Madame Moldo a smile in reply.

'Very pleased to meet you,' I said.

She smoothed her sweater over her bosom in an efficient sort of way. I would learn over the ensuing months that she nurtured an unbounded passion for mohair, in every colour under the sun, plain or cabled, threaded through with gold, silver or feathers. Here was a woman who appreciated the smoothness of the keys on her computer keyboard, who took pleasure in articulating each word that she pronounced with great clarity, and in making sure that her lumbar vertebrae were properly supported by the ergonomic backrest of her chair.

'Shall I put that in the minutes, Monsieur Moldo?'

'Absolutely, Madame Moldo.'

I am grateful to them for this little display they put on for us, calling each other by their surname, and I admire their administrative zeal. I intend to become obsessed with these little manias of theirs. Otherwise I'm quite sure I could die of boredom.

'We're very lucky in this building, no, I mean it, very lucky,' Monsieur Moldo insisted, almost bent double over his desk in an eminently persuasive posture. 'Because there are no tenants. And that's very unusual. Ex-cep-tio-nal. All our good co-owners actually live in the building and that's why they take such an active interest in the joint ownership itself. Monsieur and Madame Dupotier send apologies for absence, they are both very ill and have become very frail; do you have their authority, Madame Pognon? Make a note of that, Madame Moldo: Madame Pognon has the Dupotiers' authority to give their vote by proxy. The Kovaks are not here but they won't have a proxy vote, they're behind with their maintenance charges by . . . let me see . . . very nearly eight months now, but, well, don't let's get too panicky, their daughter has rung me from Washington. Make a note, Madame Moldo: Kovaks absent, no proxy vote, send them two more reminders, then the blue form – if that's what they want, they shall have it. No, I'm joking, we've never yet had to resort to the bailiffs. Isn't that so, Madame Moldo?'

I look around me, envisage all the old blood flowing through my neighbours' bodies. We've moved into a hospice.

Monsieur and Madame Pognon. He looks like an under-taker and wears rather delicate, Italian-style leather shoes. He's very tall and very thin, with a beautiful pearly grey complexion. His wife, whom I've met quite a few times on the stairs, never recognises me. She always looks rather like a frightened chicken, with a short but very substantial body.

She probably only comes up to his sternum. I think I am right in saying they have a linen and bedding shop; unimaginable, like trying to tell me that my own parents run a chain of sex-shops.

'So you're against the pigeon net, Madame Jauffret?'

'Yes, I stand by my decision.'

'Could you justify it for us?'

'Monsieur Moldo, you are perfectly well aware that, as I live on the top floor, I have the benefit of unrestricted views over the whole of Paris, and that my bathroom window looks towards Sacré-Coeur, so try and imagine the effect if someone went and put a great net over . . .'

Madame Jauffret slows down, she suffers from asthma or something like that, which means she has difficulty breathing. She collapses onto herself and seems to fall asleep half way through her sentence.

Madame Dïstik really has fallen asleep, still in her headscarf and with her handbag clamped between her crossed arms. Her husband is heaving great sighs of exasperation. They are the same size as each other with the same eyes and the same jackets.

Madame Calmann gives me a little wave. She's my favourite neighbour, the only one who says hello to me. Her hair is always impeccably set and her little dog perfectly silent. She often talks about her husband, in lowered tones, with her eyes raised to the heavens, because he's too fat and refuses to diet. Monsieur Calmann must be mounted on a cushion of air. Despite his size, he never makes a sound. Perhaps that's thanks to his exercises. He has a personal trainer, paid for by Social Security, who helps him do them.

I've lived in several buildings in my time, never in a tower block, but in places that counted up to sixteen flats. As a child, I never really grasped the complex notion of what a neighbour was. I would meet people on the stairs who invariably noticed that I had grown. The children my age were of little interest to me; we went to different schools and therefore might as well have lived on different planets. This apartment, the one we bought two months ago, is my first real home, and I've decided to behave like a responsible woman.

To give the right impression, I cross one knee over the other. I adopt this posture cautiously: ever since I first set eyes on this world, ever since, with all my childish worldliness, I first started watching how grown-ups behave, I've noticed that this was top of their list of favourite positions. Men and women alike cross one knee over the other. It's bad for the back, but it's good for the ego. You immediately feel more respectable. I therefore cross my legs like a good girl, and notice the perfect harmony it produces between myself and Madame Pétronie, who's sitting next to me in the same position. Madame Pétronie is a small woman of about sixty, immaculately turned out, and with a remarkably kindly eye. Her husband, on the other hand, looks seriously out of place.

He has very short arms so that his hands are drowned in the excess length of sleeve in his suit. He hasn't crossed his knees. He can't because he's not quite normal. I can't think of another way of saying it. His face constantly contorts into grimaces, afflicted by endless tics and twitches. He makes a strange noise with his mouth, the kind of noise people make to cats or chickens or sheep, a sort of loud, repeated kissing sound. Because we're all nicely brought up, we all behave as if we find this perfectly normal. In our community of healthy individuals we accept him as he is.

I wonder what exactly Madame Pétronie can have been thinking when she married Monsieur Pétronie. Perhaps he was not so damaged as a young man, not so strange. It was probably because of some illness, and it makes me terribly sad to think of his gradual deterioration to this present state, like a grumpy, ageing baby. But it's even more sad to think he might always have been like this, and that Madame Pétronie selected him in spite of everything, not because he was rich – which he genuinely was, I think – but because she wanted to do something good. She gathered him up in her love (for I must point out that she displays sincere affection for him at all times). She must have been paying for some appalling sin. I imagine her forty years earlier. She would have been quite pretty in a rather unusual way, pretty but marked by the ladleful of boiling contrition poured over her youthful head. Perhaps that's what Christianity is, I tell myself. This unnatural decision to choose the weakest, to love the most

7

defenceless, to give one's life to appease the suffering of others.

'Do you know if it's a boy or a girl?'

Madame Pétronie is leaning towards me. She whispered this in my ear and gazed at my tummy with a gentle, moist expression which instantly softens me. I hesitate before replying, afraid I'll be reprimanded for unauthorised chatting. I shake my head to show that I don't.

'I've got a son,' she says.

Ouch, I think. Well, that can't be a pretty sight. But her shining eyes assure me to the contrary. Her son is her victory, the risk she took against all the odds, and won. Always trust people's expressions – a fair and unequivocal law.

Over the next week I met them both, in the street, mother and son, a sumptuous man, irreproachably normal, flagrantly upright. He held the front door open for me, elegantly and gallantly allowing me to go in ahead of him. The official shiver that ran down my back informed me that I thought he was to die for.

'Let's get on with it, Madame Moldo, the motion for the net is carried by eight votes to one. Madame Jauffret, please . . .'

'It's my right to express my opinion.'

'But you can see for yourself that it's pointless, it's going to go up anyway.'

'It's my right,' repeated Madame Jauffret, almost apoplectic.

Madame Pétronie and I exchange a doubtful glance. Should we intervene? Monsieur Créton doesn't give us the opportunity.

'As chairman of the management committee,' he announces in a falsetto voice, 'I would like to point out that my neighbour's attitude, although not very constructive, is perfectly legal and well-founded. Permit me nevertheless, my dear Madame Jauffret, to remind you now that in response to the letter dated the eleventh of this month . . .'

Monsieur Moldo closes his eyes. His punishment for the day is upon him, and he decides to endure its agonies quietly. I turn to see who's talking, who has the unusual gift to make themselves so disagreeable and so boring in just two sentences. The tide of Monsieur Créton's rhetoric cannot be staunched. He quotes willy-nilly from various articles in the building's code of agreement, and refers back to extracts from the minutes of earlier meetings. He has a mania for administrative detail. His wife, a burly, obese bull-mastiff of a woman with slightly bulging eyes, digs him repeatedly in the ribs with her elbows while he pours the completely meaningless flow of his argument over his listeners. Contrary to normal expectations, the digging elbows are not intended to make him shut up, but to encourage him. Adroitly manipulated by this form of remote-control, he continues to croak amid our collective indifference.

Every one of them will end up speaking out about something, even Madame Distik will wake up to put her oar in.

To them, it isn't a question of adding any meaning to the proceedings, of making a point any more clearly understood; it's to do with expressing the rather confused version of the truth that lies sealed in each of their hearts. A hospice, yes, and a lunatic asylum as well, I think as I look at my watch. Two hours have passed already and we've only reached the second point on the agenda which runs to five points.

Julien has crossed his hands and rests his chin on them. It looks as if he finds it all very amusing. This is the beginning of our new life, I tell myself.

I was full of hope and determination when I moved into number 116/118 on that boulevard.

2

A Fascinating Bosom

Christmas is nearly upon us, a fertile season for nervous breakdowns and despair.

Monsieur Dupotier has just come to see me. It's the third time this morning. His visits are becoming more and more frequent.

I don't give a damn about Christmas, even though not giving a damn at Christmas requires an effort of uninterrupted concentration over a period of about two months.

He does give a damn. He thinks about it, he sees it on TV. He remembers it, with his dog, his wife and his son. All three of them have died, one after the other.

The dog led the cortège. I'd been living in the building for barely three months, but already knew the Dupotiers: it took them hours to get up to and down from their apartment. Blacky, the cocker spaniel, was no speedier – he seemed to be sort of knock-kneed (although I don't know whether this is a recognised malformation in dogs), in any event he made rather painful progress, his belly almost scraping the ground and his paws splayed in an X shape. He was such a pitiful creature that, compared to him, Monsieur and Madame Dupotier looked almost like spring chickens.

So the dog died first. I didn't learn how and didn't find out straight away. Despite my vigilance, or perhaps because of it, news always takes a little time to reach me.

Madame Dupotier was on the stairs, halfway between two floors, clinging to the banister rail. Was she waiting for Blacky?

'Our poor little doggie's dead, my dear.'

I wondered whether they had had him buried. I put on the appropriate sympathetic expression. I would have liked to take her hand, but I didn't dare.

Madame Dupotier had long thin fingers which looked hooked and chalky. This last characteristic could in fact have been applied to all of her person. Every time I saw her coming out of her apartment, I was astonished by how white she was. There was something dusty about this whiteness, as if the whole building had collapsed on top of her and she had miraculously emerged unscathed, and the only sign of her ordeal was this plastery film penetrating her every pore.

If I didn't shake her hand it was also because I'm frightened of old ladies. Isn't there a story about a young girl who goes to fetch water from the fountain and offers her jug to the old lady? Well, I would have failed. Seeing her there by the water, bent double, all skin and bone, with watery red eyelids, I would have run in the opposite direction. I don't actually like touching people in general. I'm afraid they'll take it the wrong way or find it unsettling.

After Blacky's death, the grocer downstairs asked whether the Dupotiers would like to have one of his puppies, but they told him that they didn't want to orphan the poor creature. They felt they'd come to the end of the road. Which, in Madame Dupotier's case, constituted an impressive demonstration of clairvoyance: she took less than six months to go.

This time I was the first to know. Monsieur Dupotier came and knocked on my door.

'Oh, my dear, if you only knew. Something terrible's happened.'

I would like to have taken *his* hand then, too. But he was even more off-putting than his wife, because he'd given up cutting his fingernails and they were going black and beginning to dig into the grey flesh around them. I couldn't help looking at them every time I saw him, because it struck me that they provided reliable evidence that, as time went by, humans reverted to an animal state.

Two days later the *gardienne*, the woman who was our caretaker, rang at the door.

'D'you want to come and see the body?'

I didn't understand straight away. Simone, the *gardienne*, has always addressed me in this unusually familiar way. I absolutely must tell you why. I absolutely must tell you about Simone – in fact I wonder whether that's where I should have started.

Telling you about Simone inevitably means telling you

about myself. Not because we're especially alike, but because she came into my life so easily.

When I first came to see the apartment, I felt that I'd found my home. This was where I wanted to live. This was where our child would be born. They were asking too much money but there was no going back. It was love at first sight.

The deal was done and we moved in two months later. I was pregnant and therefore let off the heavy work. I lay full length on the long oak table that the previous occupants had left behind, and waited for the arrival of the cardboard boxes. It was a lovely day. The window was open. I was thinking: 'I'm never going to be able to live here, there's too much noise.' I felt like crying because I knew there was no way of turning back the clock. I tried to convince myself that it wasn't really noisy, that it just seemed noisy.

When I got up to close the window, there was Simone, standing in front of me.

'The door was open, so I came in,' she said.

She didn't make me jump, I was too intrigued by the way she looked to be surprised that she was there in the first place.

'Simone, the *gardienne*.'

'Sonia . . . I'm the new owner.'

'Sonia, you look as if you're pregnant.'

I looked down at my tummy, which was slightly smaller than hers.

Simone was quite fat although that word doesn't do justice

to her general appearance. Carrying her bulky trunk was a pair of lean, muscly legs. And above her admirably rounded abdomen rested her opulent breasts. She was short and her head sat squat on her shoulders. But her face and her arms were nicely formed. Ageing, flabby and blotchy, but nicely formed. Her hair was her pride and joy. It was lovingly peroxided, and fell to her shoulders in layers of gleaming curls. When she smiled she revealed, amazingly, that practically every other tooth was missing. Her lips were slightly deformed where they had moulded to the stumps and, instead of being made-up in red, they were pale and chapped, which was more in keeping with her pasty complexion – slightly marbled on her cheek-bones and almost green in the hollows beneath them – and her rough skin than her 1950s Hollywood hairstyle. She usually wore a pair of worn-out old slippers and a blouse unbuttoned far enough to expose her fascinating bosom.

'Yes,' I replied. 'I'm nearly seven months.'

She delved through her pockets, brought out an old till receipt and a pencil and then, leaning on the table, prepared to make some notes.

'National Health number. Your mother's name and telephone number. Your mother-in-law's name and telephone number.'

I enumerated the details without hesitating. As soon as I finished a wave of panic swept over me. Perhaps she was from the police.

I was often frightened that I was going to be arrested. When Julien and I were driving perfectly legally along the road I would say: 'Careful, the police!'

Perhaps she was a fascist. She would inform on us. To whom? That was certainly a valid question, but my mind doesn't work like that. I mean, there's no room for logic in me. Every available bit of space is inhabited by fear.

'What does your husband do?'

'He's an architect.'

I had no right to do that. Revealing things about myself was probably a mistake, but divulging information about Julien was going too far. He would never forgive me.

'Architects travel a lot,' she said, straightening up, putting her hands on her hips and pulling a face. 'Just think if the baby comes while your man's away somewhere.'

I shrugged, speechless.

'I pop you in a taxi, send you to hospital and I ring your mother and your mother-in-law so that they can take care of everything. Give me a set of your keys to that I can open up for them if there's an emergency. If your waters break, you wouldn't have time to pack your suitcase.'

I couldn't disagree.

I handed her a set of keys which she immediately stowed in her pocket. The clinking sounds and the bulge in the fabric indicated that she was in possession of a repertoire of keys that would have put a jailer to shame.

'Right then, I'll let you get on. If you need anything, just give me a shout and I'll come running. If you need someone to clean up, there's my cousin Josette. Moving house is always a messy business. I'll tell her to come by tomorrow. Would ten o'clock be all right?'

Without waiting for my reply, she turned on her heel and disappeared.

Sitting on the only piece of furniture in my new apartment, I tried for a moment to persuade myself that it had been a dream.

If events ever get on top of me, or if something shocking or violent happens, I tend to take a step back from life. I let it happen and wait for it to pass. Julien maintains that it's the Ostrich Policy, the way cowards avoid meeting reality head on. How can I defend myself against that? He's right, I know he is, but I can't do anything about it.

On the days when I'm feeling really good, those mornings when a vindictive force flows through my veins instead of the usual insipid blood, I take pleasure in perceiving the way I deal with problems as a secret kind of heroism. It's true that, thanks to this aforementioned method, I can end up in the kind of mess that more courageous, even intrepid, characters would have fled without a moment's hesitation.

It's at times like that that I feel good about myself. I believe that I am commendably curious about life and that I'm ready to risk my very well-being and – perhaps, yes, it has to be admitted – even other people's, in order to further my knowledge and understanding of the world.

Simone, on one of those good days, seemed to me like the subject of a daring experiment on human behaviour in a hostile environment: living in 15 square metres with a dog, a couple of budgerigars and the stench of twelve days' dirty dishes, set against a backdrop of 24-hour TV blaring out at 90 decibels.

On the darker days, she wore a quite different face. That was when I realised my own weakness, amazed at my capacity for allowing this sort of intruder to have access to the intimacy of my own home.

When her cousin Josette turned up the following morning with a slimy bucket in her hand and a ravaged old floor cloth over her shoulder, I could see the full extent of my fecklessness.

But it was in Julien's expression that I read the full impact of this particular brand of madness which, when it takes hold of me, leaves me as weak and aimless as a bit of seaweed tossed and carried by the currents.

He could see Josette as she really was: an angular woman with flinty knees, dirty toes sticking out of the end of her orthopaedic sandals, a long conical nose, prying eyes and black teeth. There was something disturbing about her, something surreptitious about the way she looked at you, and she carried with her an unpleasant smell of roll-up Gitanes.

Julien asked me, 'Who the hell is that?'

I realised that 'the cleaning woman' was not the right answer.

'Josette, Simone's cousin.'

'And who's Simone.'

'The *gardienne* for this building.'

Julien smiled. I was saved. He hates me and he loves me for exactly the same reasons – which doesn't make life easy for him.

So, I'd got to Madame Dupotier's death, and to her body, which I had to go and see. Simone stood on the doormat, with her hands burrowing into her pockets, looking at me. She had moist, drooping eyes, and her head was slightly on one side. She looked like a dog, which immediately made me think of Blacky, and of a possible reincarnation. That's the sort of idiotic idea that wafts through my head all day long. I thought she looked rather beautiful with her gentle, tentative smile. More than anything else I felt that her presence meant something to me, the simple fact of her existence was important to me because she was such an improbable character. Before I met Simone, I didn't know people like her existed.

I admit to having a self-contradictory relationship with reality. I'm usually not convinced by what is served up to me each morning – I mean the world, the sky, the sounds of the city outside. I spend a good part of each day scrutinising some obscure point on this early perspective looking for a sign, something different, some proof that there's something else, that we've been on the wrong tack all along. I feel ready to accept the most insignificant discovery. Tell me that the world is not, after all, as round as all that and I'll give you a year's supply of your favourite biscuits. In fact what I'm waiting for is confirmation of my intuition: we can't possibly know everything; and that's exactly why we just don't get the most important point of all, which is what makes it so difficult to get up in the mornings. What's the point if everything is false, incomplete, an illusion. Give me three aliens from Venus, a carnivorous plant that can swallow a whole buffalo, proof that a significant proportion of a hippopotamus's brain is devoted to sustaining flight . . . and I'll rest easy at night. There's so much chaos around me, so much disorder and absurdity, and I have to pretend to believe what I'm told . . .

But I digress, I just wanted to say that I really liked her, Simone, this improbable Simone who was standing there in front of me on my door mat and saying, 'Come and see the body. I'm going. I already saw it yesterday, but I'm going back again. She's very peaceful, you'll see. Such a lovely face she had, our Madame Dupotier.'

I didn't know what to say to this. I was afraid of going, and I couldn't see what good it would do anyone. I thought of telling Simone that my religion forbade me from making this sort of visit, but on the one hand I wasn't sure whether this was true and on the other hand I wasn't sure that I wanted to get onto that sort of subject with her. Mind you, a few weeks after we'd moved into the apartment she'd said,

'I get on with everyone. Take the butcher downstairs, for example, I buy my meat from him. It's kosher, but I couldn't care less.'

There was indeed a butcher's shop on the ground floor of our building. Monsieur Lakrach smiled a great deal and actually sold Halal meat. As far as Simone was concerned, Moslems and Jews were all much of a muchness, which proved that she wasn't racist.

'No thanks, Simone. I don't want to.'

'It would make the old man happy if you went.'

I pictured Monsieur Dupotier, a puny figure in his corduroy trousers, his floppy tie untidily knotted round his stringy neck, joining his hands as he sat at his dead wife's bedside. I didn't have the strength to face this scene. And I knew myself too well to take the risk.

Confronted with Madame Dupotier's body, I would probably have started to count the hairs sprouting from the widower's ear holes. The room would be steeped in shadows, cluttered with useless defunct belongings, abandoned, stagnating in a layer of dirt, and I would sniff noisily, offended by the sickening smell of the place where the windows were always conscientiously closed for fear of draughts. It smelt so horrible in their apartment.

At the time, I had never actually been through their door, but every time I had the ill luck to be passing when they opened it, a sweetish stench would stick in my throat. Then I couldn't help myself wallowing in it, in my puerile masochistic way, taking a great lungful of it to identify the components of the disgusting smell. Rancid redhead, leeks swimming in cooking water, overripe fruit, musty bedding stuffed with mothballs waiting to be washed. All that and much more sculpted by a film of filth and condemned to slow decomposition.

'I can't,' I replied feebly. 'The baby's about to wake up.'

That was a lie. Moses had only just gone to sleep.

'I'll keep an eye on him if you want,' said Simone.

How could I refuse? Lending your baby, I had soon discovered, constituted a demonstration of affection and friendship as well as tangible proof of a generosity and magnanimity of spirit, all feelings after which I strove desperately so as to be forgiven my unmentionable sins. Lending your baby helped to reinforce social links, it sometimes even created them. Such was the line of argument I rammed down my own throat to overcome my reticence.

That's all about smells too. Moses just had to spend a few minutes in someone else's arms and he came back to me quite different, smelling of Aunt Thingummy or Uncle Whatsit. If his godfather Eloi with the luxuriant red beard got hold of him, it took me a while to shake off the idea that my baby too had the beard, so powerfully did the well-meaning giant's smell decant onto his smooth head. That's why I would smile privately if my son screamed when a stranger picked him up. Don't misunderstand me, my happiness wasn't fuelled by the rejection that so devastated these others. It was far more organic. As soon as Moses started to cry, his head was bathed in a veil of sweat, immediately restoring his delicious, incomparable aroma.

Moses embalmed in Simone's drunken breath, stroked by her nicotine-stained fingers, lulled against her bosom, that fascinating bosom which she used as storage space, a purse in which she stashed notes and coins, and as a sewing box. The damage would be irreparable. You didn't know what might be hiding in that deep crevasse between her breasts!

The telephone rang and, shutting the door on Simone – who was more understanding than I would have predicted – I was surprised to find myself thanking a god in whom I didn't believe.

3

Such a Lovely Place

Three years have passed. I have a second child, a new baby called Nestor who smells exactly like Julien, a coincidence which absolutely delights me. I work from nine till noon every morning, translating a worthy theorist's book about the revival of the Anglican church. I understand absolutely nothing about the sentences I spew out on my computer screen, but I know that they're right, because English is perfectly transparent to me. It's as if I'm gazing into a pool of clear water and can see a procession of fish swimming past; moments earlier I didn't even know they existed but I can now draw them freehand without missing a single detail or the least nuance of colour.

My husband is in Caen, on his first real building project: an annexe to the municipal library which he will raise from a grassy mound like a rabbit from a hat. It's going to be long, low and white, hard up against the existing building and linked in with it. He's shown me what it'll be like by building a miniature version with matchboxes. I clapped. We set up a spot-light on one side to represent the sun, and for clouds, I ran my fingers in and out of the ray of light.

'It'll never be that pretty in real life,' he said.

Julien is always rather sad. He is always prepared for fail-
ure, and that is his strength. I feel safe with him because I
know that life can never be as ugly as it is in his nightmares.

Perhaps I'm wrong.

I can just see him, with his orange hard hat flattening his
fringe over his eyes. The early days are the worst. The project
managers never take him seriously. Whatever he does – and
this terrible fate must have been cast on him by some sprite
or a witch – Julien looks about fourteen-and-a-half.

I miss him, but I make the most of his absence by indulging
my whims. I make everything warm and comfortable around
me, I listen to trashy songs on the radio, and I pass the time
of day with the shopkeepers on the boulevard.

Now, that's what's changed the most in three years. The
boulevard, I mean.

When we arrived here, it was a pitiful place, strewn with
old newspapers and bottle tops, and dotted with clusters of
broken-down refrigerators topped off with the rusting drums
of ancient washing machines. A stained old mattress would
sometimes come to complete these random constructions.
All these things lying around discarded like that made me
feel sad. I thought of the people who had used them, carried
on using them till the bitter end; they spoke to me of difficult,
dingy lives. Metal shutters were drawn down over the shops
that had gone bankrupt. Abandoned bars – dark, narrow,
joyless places – played host to the unemployed, a few Arabs
who had traded in their work overalls for suits made in

Shanghai. Everyone eyed everyone else suspiciously: the shop-keepers, survivors from the Auvergne who had made it up to the city, were filled with sickening disappointment, and the immigrants with fear and – yes – dignity. This dignity that the papers talked about as if it were some sort of surprise, a trinket, a chance occurrence, which, if they were to be believed, was almost decorative.

I could go out in my slippers and dressing-gown. Well, why not – I felt protected from stares and judgements. Not in contention. I was a timorous witness to squabbles carried out as people hurried along the pavement, to sudden bursts of anger on the street, to murderous thoughts that broke my heart, as I trailed the shopping trolley behind me with my first new-born baby in a sling on my belly, on the look out. I heard everything: 'We've got enough of their sort round here', 'They let their little nigger children run about all over the place', 'I've never had a problem with the Chinese, it's the others'. Could I go on behaving like an ostrich for ever? My head in the sand, my favourite sport. But there wasn't any sand on the boulevard.

More than once I actually abandoned a whole kilo of tomatoes in front of the shopkeeper in 'Fresh From My Orchard' because of some abject comment he'd uttered from those podgy jowls.

Is that the only feat of arms chalked up in your heroic rebellion, brave Sonia?

I'm afraid it is. I sensed terrifying violence, endless misery, infinite resignation, and I had only one response: to think about when I was little, when things were not so bad and when, anyway, I didn't know about anything except for my mother's warm arms when I woke up.

On polling days, the cast iron lid that weighed down on my head would lift just a few centimetres. I would trip happily across the deserted school playground to the polling booths as if they were temples of happiness, the last refuge of wisdom. Then the lid would fall back down again, sometimes more heavily than others.

'Well, what do you expect?' Julien would ask me.

I expect people to be happy, but I dare not say it because I know that, yet again, it's my own weakness speaking.

In the summer it was different. At last the flip-flops the West Africans wore seemed appropriate. I no longer had to worry about their toes being covered with chilblains. The heat and the sun at least justified their enforced idleness too. What could be nicer than to unfold a garden chair on the wide pavement and read the sports pages under the shady acacia trees with their soft green leaves? A gentle breeze swept through the swaying branches and you might catch yourself trying to see the sea somewhere in the distance. The temperature only had to go up to 20°C and you could think you were in Marseilles. The children playing in the streets no longer looked abandoned, they were free, and the fact that they had no socks suddenly became a blessing. Every time I left these heights to go into the city, I felt sorry for the smart boys in their Bermuda shorts and lace-up shoes, the girls with tight collars on their dresses and patent leather shoes on their feet, and the swaddled babies crying in their push-chairs with ineffectual parasols which didn't protect them from the scorching heat.

But, as I was saying, the boulevard has changed a great deal in three years. I couldn't put a date on it. The first signs passed unnoticed. Then one day, I was no longer the only person sitting out on the terrace at the Bar des Alouettes. I looked up shyly at the new customers. They were reading *Libération*, not the usual *Le Parisien*, and they ordered buttered bread as well as their little cups of black coffee; they wore over-sized jeans and shirts unbuttoned to reveal faded T-shirts, monstrously expensive trainers on their feet, and smiles on their faces that betrayed peace of mind, they didn't have to worry about any contingencies other than the sheer pleasure of relaxing. Quite often they cluttered the little white tables with their notebooks and their pens. They were authors or screenwriters. The girls were incredibly pretty. What is it with girls' bodies now? Some new gimmick. They have large breasts and lean thighs which slot perfectly into their narrow hips. These girls were actresses. Their smiles were so wide, they took up their whole faces. They moved their hands languidly about their faces. They rolled their eyes, lowered them, then closed them for a moment. They behaved as if the camera wasn't even there, except that there wasn't a camera. They talked loudly and they were amusing. They made the boys laugh as they lolled in their chairs, with their feet up, making sure they were cool, very, very cool. I felt about ninety years old. I stopped going to the Bar des Alouettes. I took to having my cup of coffee back at home once I'd dropped Moses at school.

Two years later I would read a magazine article about the metamorphosis of the area. Following the crash in property prices in the outer arrondissements of Paris, the young chose to set up home further from the centre. A friendly, colourful crowd had come to brighten up the evenings in Belleville, and the bar terraces didn't start emptying until two o'clock in the morning. As is often the case, I didn't really know how I felt about it.

I wonder what other people do. As soon as I cast judgement on something in my mind, a brigade of heavily armed neurones organise a counter-offensive. All I'm good for is stating the facts. I notice that the atmosphere feels curdled in there some days, like a bowl of milk with a drop of lemon juice in it.

It's what is known in politics as cohabitation, I think. I don't know why, but it plunges me into a state of profound confusion. Probably because I find it difficult to determine which camp I'm in or to recognise our smallest common denominator. More often than not, all I can see in it is a tragic lack of understanding. I feel like a balloon drifting from one person to the next, caught, held, then thrown up again. I understand, yes, I understand everything, and I understand all of them: the French, because I've read Balzac, Victor Hugo and Flaubert; the Arabs because I was cradled as a baby to the voice of Oum Kalsoum; the Vietnamese because I know my fair share about genocidal suffering; the Jews because I am one; and the Catholics thanks to Flannery O'Connor. I identify with all of them without ever actually feeling at home or at ease with any of them. They are all both alien and familiar, because I'm not entirely French, nor any more Arab, certainly not Vietnamese, only slightly Jewish and even less Catholic. I stay on the periphery. I can laugh about it, and I don't expect some impossible reconciliation. I laugh about it like that day at the chemists when I identified alternately with two Jewish boys from the Yeshiva school, and a stunning beauty, the glittering froth skimmed from the *bouillon* of Paris fashion.

The dispensary is full to bursting. All the customers keep shifting their weight from one foot to the other so as not to get cramp. They can't relax for a moment because, on top of the suffocating heat in the shop, they're consumed with the fear that someone might shuffle ahead of them in the queue. They watch each other, throwing each other apparently friendly glances, which are actually full of suspicion. Then two young Orthodox Jews and a beautiful woman with big hair reach the counter at exactly the same moment. The two exhausted pharmacists behind the counter start asking them questions. The two young Jews don't speak very good French; it's a long painful wait for the people behind them.

I can feel a wave of anti-Semitism rising in the ranks. On the other hand, they're talking to each other in impeccable English, and I listen delightedly. I'm about to intervene in this transaction when the other customer catches my eye, the one with big hair. The pharmacist is asking her how she's coping with the heat. She must be a regular customer and they must feel they can't just stamp her prescription form without making some semblance of conversation. The woman with the splendid hair thinks for a while before answering. I'm not sure why, but I wait for her answer with bated breath. If, when it comes to it, I have to trample over one of my kin to hear her more clearly, I wouldn't hesitate for a moment. And I'm justified, because when she does speak, I'm richly rewarded.

She says, 'The heat doesn't bother me. I've learned to live with it. I hardly even notice the streams of sweat running down my body. They're just doing their job.' The pharmacist gives her an embarrassed smile. She's never heard anything like it. 'Streams of sweat', now what would that look like? I'm quite sure, on the other hand, that the two Jews know exactly what she means. Firstly because, dressed as they are in their traditional fringed tunics, shirts done up to the chin, black jackets, and woollen coats they're familiar with this sort of flow of water. But also because, in their life of abstinence, their ears are finely tuned to every desire, and their imaginations are quick to understand. As for me, even though I don't live a life of abstinence and I'm wearing a backless dress, I'm overcome with emotion at her words. I can feel the streams of sweat running down my own body, and I'm thrilled by them. I don't know how to thank this Parisienne with the ridiculous hair who's given me this moment of pure pleasure.

So I was saying that I'm making everything warm and comfortable around me: Moses will be sitting cross-legged in the playground at nursery school, singing *Ten Green Bottles*, while Nestor makes indecipherable little whimpers, lying limply in my arms with his eyes half closed. I look out of the window at the pollarded acacia in the courtyard, which has never actually been trimmed.

Monsieur Créton, our neighbour from the fourth floor, and chairman of our management committee, contributed to the removal of the ancient chestnut tree which, according to him, was robbing our homes of light with its profuse foliage. 'A pollarded acacia tree is more distinguished and at least it can be controlled. It will never grow above the first floor.' The day the old tree was uprooted, it was appallingly hot and when the bulldozer crushed the trunk between its jaws to finish off the job, the heart of the tree let out a mournful wail that brought tears to my eyes.

Now I can take consolation from the fact that our dear neighbour's predictions were completely ridiculous. The pollarded acacia, that dear little dwarf tree, moved by some bizarre sense of vegetable pride, has already reached the second floor and its indomitable boughs come and tickle the forged iron railings of my balcony on the first floor.

I congratulate myself on this subtle rebellion, and I'm wondering how I might describe it to my exiled beloved, when the doorbell rings. I put Nestor down in his cradle, taking care not to wake him, and make my way slowly over to the door, imagining some wonderful surprise: a bouquet of roses from Caen, a cheque from my editor . . .

It's Monsieur Dupotier.

In striped pyjamas, standing in front of me, thin as a heron and looking disorientated. His hands shake as he squeezes them against each other, and his head totters dangerously on his neck.

'I've lost my son,' he says.

I didn't know he had one. It's a sort of hello/goodbye only sadder. He's standing motionless, staring at me with great round eyes, and I wonder if he isn't actually going mad. I vaguely know the story of his life. His brother was the archi-tect who designed our apartment building, and he's always lived in it. At twenty-five he inherited the hardware shop in the rue Ménilmontant, which has been walled up for as long as I've known it. It's a tiny house with a pointed roof, straight out of a children's book. On the shop-front, above the windows that are now blinded by a wall of breeze blocks, a curved sign still makes the obsolete claim 'we sell colour'. All his life, the drab Monsieur Dupotier, with his eyelids like crinkled brown paper, sold colours. I briefly imagine the late Madame Dupotier behind the counter, her head still boasting

SUCH A LOVELY PLACE

all the beautiful hair she had lost, counting the bank notes with her long bony hands and making each coin chink in the drawer of the till, while her husband piled tins of paint right up to the ceiling. It's never occurred to me that they could have any descendants. That's probably why Blacky's death affected me so much. When the dog died, I told myself that that was the most heartbreaking thing that could happen to them.

'How old was he?' I asked, more to provoke some sort of reaction in the inert old man than out of curiosity.

'Sixty, my dear. He had a heart attack.'

I wanted Julien to come back straight away, I wanted him to spring up beside me out of the floorboards so that he could take the situation in hand. He would probably have known just what to say, prepared as he was for such a variety of catastrophes. My own optimism was disarmed.

'Come on,' I said, 'I'll take you back home.'

I took Monsieur Dupotier by the arm. Having checked that the keys to my apartment were safe in the bottom of my pocket, I closed the door, praying that Nestor wouldn't wake up.

At about the speed of a funeral procession, we crossed the landing. Monsieur Dupotier's head kept nodding and shaking. I went in to his apartment, my tummy gripped with fear, as if I had suddenly changed places with Blue-beard's wife as she stood on the threshold of the forbidden room. Within these colourless walls, in the mute confines of

35

these carpets, beneath the dim rays of sunlight that filtered through the dirty curtains, death had decided to strike once more.

I knew that the son didn't live with his parents; and yet I couldn't help feeling afraid that I might come across his ghost each time we passed a doorway. Without knowing which of us was leading the other, we ended up in the bedroom. Most of the room was taken up by a huge bed made of dark wood, strewn with tumbling eiderdowns and corkscrewed sheets. Monsieur Dupotier lay down. I helped him put his feet up, without actually dredging up the courage to take off his old slippers, and I wondered whether he too had decided his time had come. What if he dies right now, what should I do? Close his eyelids like on TV?

'I'm cold,' he said in a reedy little voice.

I pulled one of the blankets free and put it over his body.

'You wouldn't put the boiler on for me, would you?'

'But it's June, Monsieur Dupotier.'

Couldn't I think of anything better to say to him? Anything more comforting?

'Oh, I'm so cold.'

I left him a moment to go into the kitchen. His apartment was an exact replica of my own. Except that in mine, the air was transparent, the walls were white and the parquet was golden.

The kitchen was worse than the rest. When I pushed the door open, an army of cockroaches thought of beating a retreat and then decided against it. Their instinct to flee, I thought – how strange to be wondering what goes on inside a cockroach! But in the circumstances it was quite entertaining – their instinct to flee was giving in to their understanding of the situation: nothing to worry about in an old man who was half blind and who'd long since perceived them as part of the pattern on the wallpaper. These creatures were obviously not wily enough to realise that this tall figure by the sink was actually me, but it didn't make any difference. I was more terrified by their tiniest antenna than they would have been by fifty demijohns of insecticide.

I unfocused my eyes so that I could no longer see them swarming and could summon the courage to lift my arm up towards the on-off tap on the boiler. The switch, which had a little picture of a flame on it, was so sticky with grime that I retched. I looked away while my disgusted fingers turned the long screw on its axis. How could I have guessed that right next to it, but a little lower down, in the place that I had chosen to look so as not to be overcome with nausea, there was a stack of dirty washing-up? It was all beginning to go green, bits of food had encrusted themselves onto the sponge which had, at some point, tried to tackle the job; a veil of grey dust made the whole edifice merge into a statuesque immutability.

I could – I should, even – have stopped at that. Pressing on the button for the gas supply, activating the little spark and, without even waiting, fleeing as far as I could go, even if it were only to my own apartment, my lovely clean apartment, which spent all its time welcoming new life, and hypothetical bouquets of flowers. It's true, that would have been abandoning the old man. But what could I do for him (except for lighting his boiler)? I would have had to start talking his language. 'My dear, what a run of bad luck. What a terrible shame, that's what I say. Your little doggy, and your good lady wife, and now your boy. Such bad luck it is.'

So I stayed in the kitchen and did what I shouldn't have done. I opened my nostrils, which I had kept hermetically sealed until then, breathed in and looked straight at that grey-green edifice.

It wouldn't be exaggerating to talk of suffocation. I thought that this, this smell, could be what had killed them one after the other.

A tiny blue flame appeared in the aperture in the boiler and I let go of the button, and leapt out of the kitchen. I really had to make an effort not to faint. A black shape, like a pool of old engine oil, was swimming before my eyes. My legs felt heavy and my heart was quivering. I was angry with myself for registering such a sight and for letting that smell inside my lungs. What on earth did my life mean if it was only separated from a life like this by walls just twenty centimetres thick? What was the point of scouring saucepans and bleaching sheets if, on the same floor, under the same roof, a scrawny exponent of my species was marinating in this melting-pot full of vermin?

That evening I tried, in a state of pitiful confusion, to make Julien understand just how helpless I felt. I had been horrible to the children. When Moses rejected his mashed potato, he saw it go flying across the kitchen. Nestor, terrified by the clatter of the plate against the wall, burst out crying before being packed off to bed before he'd even finished his bottle. They were asleep now, curled up in their beds, their backs still shuddering with the sobs that had followed their anger. I had punished them unjustly and now I was seething with rage, sharing in their indignation which had brought back to the surface memories of my own parents' episodic cruelty.

'We can't live like this,' I told Julien. 'I wish I could turn into a termite.'

'What are you going on about?'

'Insects are much more sensible than we are. There's no injustice in their world. They all help each other and they all have the same objective. They each work for the good of the whole group.'

'If you were a termite,' Julien replied kindly, 'I wouldn't be able to love you.'

He knows more than I do about animals' lives, I have to admit.

'If you were a termite,' he said again, 'you would be the queen laying her eggs, and I would just be a sterile worker who's only worried about building a good strong nest. You can't re-invent yourself. I was born to build houses.'

'Well, okay then, not a termite, if you must. Wolves then. Why can't we be wolves?'

'If I were a wolf, I'd have thirteen wives, and I don't think you'd be very happy.'

'I'm not joking.'

'Neither am I. I'm only trying to tell you that if it's love you want – and that's what you've always said you wanted – you can't go hoping for justice in the world.'

'Why does there have to be that sort of misery?'

'Why does it have to be night time? The world's just like that.'

'You're heartless.'

'Well, then you're out of luck.'

4

The Fat Pig

It's the fifth time today that Monsieur Dupotier's come to ring at the door. As I open it I have to suppress my undeniable urge to throttle him. Why's he clinging on like this? He's got nothing left to live for. His only occupation consists of working out when I come and go, and synchronising his stomach to my routine so that it rumbles at the right time. Monsieur Dupotier is hungry. From morning till night.

'You haven't got a little something have you?'

I go and find an open packet of biscuits and smile at him, hypocrite that I am.

'Thankyou, my dear,' he says in his frail voice. 'I don't know how I'd manage without you.'

You would die, I think to myself as I shake my head as if to say 'Oh, it's the least I can do, as a neighbour.'

I must give him something other than cakes and chocolate, something better than crusts of bread and the children's half eaten croissants. What he needs are hearty soups, chicken breasts, fruit and fresh dairy products. But if I start down that particular slippery slope, I'll fall all the way to the bottom. It's inevitable. I'll sit him at my table, I'll adopt him. He'll regain his strength, and he'll proclaim me a saint.

I never let him in. This rule earned me a flash of astonished admiration from Julien. I couldn't say why I felt this unequivocal sense of boundaries, of clear territorial limits. Monsieur Dupotier must not step over the threshold of our apartment under any circumstances.

The children used to wave to him expansively from the hall. They're great fans of his. They say 'Hello, Monsieur Dupotier,' in their most endearing voices; I've never seen them so polite. He's the only adult who can inspire this sort of respect in them. Nestor, who's just beginning to speak, makes colossal efforts of pronunciation to communicate with the rather deaf Monsieur Dupotier. It's so touching. I feel almost unbearably proud.

On the other hand, I try not to think too much about how stingy I'm being. I'm a very busy young woman. I work, I've got two children. There are plenty of excuses. Every time I tell friends or relations about my scrawny neighbour, people's expressions melt to a saccharine mixture of admiration and gratitude. They wouldn't be more impressed if they were talking to the Virgin Mary herself. I can see their respect for me written in their eyes. And in their silence I can hear the words they're not saying out of a sense of modesty. 'You're so good, the only person he can turn to, the only person who can make him happy even.'

I'm careful not to let my admirers know that I only give him left-overs, sugary foods full of additives, which are ruining the few teeth he's got left and are slowly finishing off a digestive system already sorely tested by the little meals Simone concocts for him every day.

Because that's the arrangement. The only heir to the Dupotier name, none other than the widow of the son who died two years ago, has arranged for the *gardienne* to bring meals up for the old man, in exchange for a meagre monthly allowance. At eleven o'clock Simone brings up a cup of white coffee and some buttered bread. At seven o'clock in the evening it's either cod and mash, or pork chop and spinach. It always smells terrible, swimming about the plate in some unidentifiable water; a scanty, pathetic meal.

I sometimes wonder why Monsieur Dupotier doesn't go out shopping. He's still strong enough. He could even eat in a restaurant, because he's not short of money either.

But he waits in the half-light of dawn, wrapped in his duvet, staring at the clock. He wakes at six. He knows he's still got five hours to wait until breakfast time. I don't know what he thinks about, what sort of dreams people his mind during the night. At about nine o'clock, having taken the children to school, Julien and I eat our croissants as we read the papers. That's when Monsieur Dupotier rings at the door for the first time each day.

He's in his pyjamas, unshaven, clasping his long fingers in a daily prayer. Sometimes, in response to some inexplicable silent negotiation, it's Julien who gets up and opens the door, with half a baguette in his hand.

'Here you are, Monsieur Dupotier. No, please. It's the least we can do.'

We don't talk about it. We've been over it all a thousand times. We've even talked about his future. We've wondered whether it wouldn't be better for him to go to an old people's home. But the woman at the pharmacy who knows all sorts of things, and not only about medicines, once said: 'Take him from his own home, and he'll die within a week. His apartment is all he's got left. It's like re-potting a sickly plant. He wouldn't have the strength to take root anywhere else.'

Monsieur Dupotier's roots. I imagined stringy white filaments twisting down the legs of his bed, boring feebly into the floorboards, the plaster and the beams as they ran out of sap, trying to reach the cellar – trickling with condensation and swarming with insects and rats – and, eventually, the ground beneath, to cling to it with microscopic brittle claws.

A few days later, there he is again. He usually has a little sleep between twelve and two. It's half past one and Monsieur Dupotier has not chosen his moment well. I'm just tearing my hair out as I scan the columns of my Harraps.

Why can I never find the word I'm looking for in the dictionary? I re-read the sentence and I know what it means. I grasp it so well I could write a dissertation about it. But there's one word that's out of reach. I've got it on the tip of my tongue. I'm hovering on the brink of it. I re-read the meanings suggested to me by the thick red tome, but they're either imprecise or too formal-sounding. Not for the first time, I feel as if I've been let down by words.

I haven't been working well recently. I'm angry because the text I'm translating, an English ethnologist's account of his travels in Polynesia, is something I would like to have written myself. I've had enough of speaking other people's words. I want to express myself. To talk about all the things I see and think, without knowing what to do with them. I think about writing poetry. As soon as I'm away from home, a thousand miles from the nearest pen or computer, I compose verses and couplets. Verbs I never use offer themselves eagerly, turns of phrase that I can't quite master arrange themselves in sophisticated systems of echoes. Whole scenes unfold. People – characters, I should say – speak to each other in me. Magnificent kisses are proffered and accepted in fields of mown corn. I come home, drunk with it. When Julien asks me what I've done with my day, I don't know what to tell him. I'd like to say 'I had a rush of inspiration,' but I'm always ashamed to. I just tell him I've been thinking. I'm grateful for the look he gives me then. A conspiratorial look. You see, he likes thinking as other people like going to football matches. It's his passion. He dreams about it at night. He takes me in his arms, inhaling along my forehead, on my hairline, as if trying to catch the smell of my thoughts. Then he lets me go with a gentle cuff on the cheek to mean 'you're my sparring-partner'.

I push my chair back violently, knocking it over so that it

clatters to the floor making an unbelievable racket. I run along the corridor, snatching a stray packet of crisps from the hall table *en route* and, in one fluid movement, I open the door and offer the crisps.

Monsieur Dupotier is standing there with his head in his hands.

When he sees the crisps he shakes his head.

'It's not that,' he says, 'it's not that.'

I didn't think there was anything else that could happen to him – he's been through everything.

'What's the matter?'

'He hit me.'

That fat pig. I'll kill him.

'He came this morning. He told me that if I didn't shave, he'd see to me.'

I notice that my neighbour's cheeks and chin are covered in grey and white hairs.

'Then what?'

'He hit me.'

'Are you hurt at all?'

'No.'

'You go home, Monsieur Dupotier. I'll take care of this.'

'Will you stand up for me?'

'Yes, I'll stand up for you.'

'Always.'

'Yes, always. Don't worry.'

He goes home. He believes me. He thinks that I'll protect him.

The fat pig. I pace round the living room. I catch sight of the Harraps, and wonder whether one good blow on the head would be enough to floor the bastard.

He arrived two months earlier. I don't know how or where from. One morning, there he was, sitting in Simone's little lodge room with just his pyjama bottoms on. I saw him through the glazed door. He's huge. He was slumped on his chair looking all bottom-heavy like a child's wobbly toy, dragging on a roll-up and stroking his great flabby stomach. His complexion was waxy, and his podgy cheeks drooped. His fat-man's breasts sprawled indecently. What little hair he had was long and brushed back, slicked back with lard. His chin jutted out like a bulldog's. The first time I saw him, I didn't actually see his eyes, he didn't look at me, and I couldn't imagine how frightened I would be when he did.

I discovered that he was Simone's brother and that she was reckoning on putting him up for a while. He's called Monsieur Pierre, but he soon became known as Simono; we think of him as an excrescence of Simone rather than as a person in his own right. He has a mad dog which he strokes ... not with his hand but with a thwack from a walking stick; and he has a silver revolver, a weapon straight out of a Western.

One morning when I was taking the rubbish down, I heard gun shots in the courtyard. I don't know what made me

47

open the door to the back of the building. I have a new kind of bravery which is growing at precisely the same rate as my children. My mission on this earth is to protect them. One shot fired in the building means the threat of a bullet somewhere. I would prefer it to get me straight away rather than have to imagine it lodging itself in my little lambs' heads.

We're standing facing each other, the fat pig and myself. He's half naked, with his gun in his hand, watching me. He doesn't make any attempt to hide it. Actually, he shows it off, rather proud of himself. He lets his gaze settle on my breasts and, for a moment, I find the idea of being a woman unbearable. His greenish eyes are like muddy puddles. With drooping jowls, he continues his perusal of my body; he looks spineless, he looks menacing, he looks like someone who's killed off a few niggers in his time, and a few Chinkies too. He swaps the gun from one hand to the other, and I tell myself he wouldn't have the balls. In the end he must have made do with informing on a few Jews, but, hey, that's pretty good going. Knowing that they were burning while he chewed on his sandwiches must have made his weekend. I'd like to be an invincible Judo black-belt, Kwaï Tchang Ken from the Kung Fu series, a little dragon like Bruce Lee, so that I could smack him in the jaw with my heel, knocking his head off, kicking his teeth out. I'd like to slice his throat open and watch him run about like a headless chicken.

'What the hell are you doing?' I ask him.

'Practising,' he replies.

'It's forbidden.'

'What's forbidden?'

'Firing like that, in an enclosed courtyard. There could be an accident.'

He comes over to me, without taking his eyes off me. His huge stomach almost touches me. The smell of his sweat infiltrates my nostrils.

'I used to be in the police,' he says with a sneaky smile playing on his lips. 'Didn't you know that, little darlin'?'

I daren't say what I'm thinking. 'Used to be, that means they chucked you out. Because you were bent, you were a disgrace to your unit.' I struggle with my old terror of the police. My arguments are buried under the avalanche of charges that could be brought against me at any moment. It wouldn't take much for me to offer him my wrists so that he could handcuff me.

I slam the door in his face. I can hear him thinking: 'Plump little chicken, frightened little spoilt bourgeois cow. She's got pretty little sweet-smelling tits, and a nice soft little arse. She's frightened of the big gun, poor 'ickle fing. Just 'cos she owns her own home, rich bitch, she thinks she can do whatever she likes.'

I go home in tears. Julien doesn't notice. I'm forced to draw attention to the fact that I'm crying by sniffing a couple of times. I cry as I tell him what's just happened, and, because he doesn't seem particularly concerned, I add: 'It's dangerous for the children. What if Moses leaned out of the window at the wrong moment. And Nestor, he's on a level with the dog's jaws. You know that dog is mad. A mad dog can kill a child.'

'It's an alarm gun.'

'What does that mean?'

'It fires blanks.'

'You can still take out someone's eye with a blank.'

'If you're a very good shot,' says Julien, laughing.

'It's not funny. He's the personification of evil, don't you understand? If you look him in the eye, it's ... horrible ...'

I start to cry again. I can't understand how Julien can carry on drawing his bloody straight lines and his sodding right-angles as if nothing's happened.

'There's evil everywhere, my darling. It's here to stay. Simono's rather pathetic. He hasn't got any balls.'

I'm saved. I know it's stupid. I look at Julien, calm and upright in front of me. He's still sitting there, bending over his drawings, but he manages to be upright all the same. It's his soul emanating from him, rising to the ceiling like an arrow. I believe. I believe he protects me.

5

Couscous

Nestor had his third birthday yesterday, and we invited sixty people to dinner. It was a mistake, but it was a good party. The next morning I have to declare the whole apartment a disaster area. There are crumbs everywhere, even inside the CD player, balloons keep popping without any warning, making me jump every time. There are cigarette butts in the soil round the house plants, and I have to convince myself that they're as good a fertiliser as any other. I estimate that it's going to take me three hours to sort the house out.

Julien left for Lille at dawn. He's transforming a disused building into a children's holiday centre. I'm not sure how he's going to go about it.

While I was trying to get to sleep he told me about Feng Shui, a set of principles devised in China for transforming hostile interiors into comfortable, balanced environments. 'You paint the corners red to neutralise the subliminal arrow shapes. You should never have windows directly opposite doors or the energy just flows straight out.' I thought I was dreaming; the occult was more my department. Or were we experiencing a case of contamination? I sank slowly into sleep, thinking of dormitories full of children in rows of beds, lying with their eyes wide open, staring at the subliminal arrows pointing at them, and praying their parents would come and pick them up first thing in the morning.

I make a courageous start in the children's bedroom, remembering the menacing motto on the wall of the library when I was at school: 'A book on the wrong shelf is a lost book.' Each toy has to be reunited with its family. If a piece of Lego ends up in the Duplo box, it's had it: no one'll go looking for it there. When I do this sort of thing, I end up thinking these inanimate objects have personalities. I find myself wanting to talk to these bits of plastic I'm handling; I want to reassure them, to tell them I'm there to make sure they get back to the right box.

There are some children's stories that can drive you mad for the rest of your days. I myself have been seriously disturbed by *The Little Tin Soldier* and *The Snow Queen*. I have to submit myself to some severe intellectual gymnastics to concede that these toy figures are no more alive than the paving stones in the street (mind you, paving stones . . .) and that a bit of dust in my eye isn't a shard of the wicked queen's broken mirror, bent on freezing my heart.

At about ten o'clock, just as I'm contemplating passing the vacuum cleaner over the left wing of our devastated palace, Monsieur Dupotier appears.

'I'm hungry, I'm so hungry.'

Galvanised by my domestic efficiency, I suddenly think of my poor neighbour as an indispensable auxiliary to my establishment. Those sixty guests didn't succeed in polishing off the couscous. For the first time since our strange nourishment-based collaboration began, I'm going to offer Monsieur Dupotier a proper meal.

'You go and sit yourself down at your table, and I'll heat you up a plate of meat and vegetables.'

I daren't tell him it was couscous. It's a lovely name, but I'm afraid of it. When I put the colourful, aromatic dish down onto the waxed cloth in front of him, I'm frightened that my guest is going to change his mind. I've already heard his sweet, gentle voice, enumerating the horrors of the Mediterranean.

'This is too much, my dear. You're too good to me.'

I can't see that there's much to boast about. Turning a fellow citizen into a dustbin has never given anyone the right to the Order of Merit. To extend the boundaries of my goodness, I decide to be stoic and sit with the old boy while he eats. I sit down opposite him and make conversation, ignoring the horrible sucking and swallowing sounds, and the trickle of broth running down his chin and staining his pyjamas. But I give up on this soon enough. I've got my housework to do, as women say in supermarket queues.

'Could you bring me the plate, when you've finished? *Bon appétit.*'

He smiles at me; there's a fine scarf of celery delicately wound round one of his long horse teeth.

As is often the case, I was right to be afraid. It was because of the couscous that everything started. I mean it was because of the couscous that everything became more serious, more sinister. Without the couscous, I might have been able to continue kidding myself with illusions of humanity.

Moses, my big six and a half-year-old Moses, is way ahead of me. Once, on election night he asked me: 'If the far right get in, will we leave straight away?' I told him: 'They won't get in.' Then he said again: 'But if they get in, we'll leave straight away, won't we? Without packing our bags.' I could read the fear in his eyes and I thought to myself that he knew more about evil than I did. He gets that from his father. He doesn't keep trying to convince himself, as his mother stupidly does, that two and two make five because it's nicer like that.

When Monsieur Dupotier brought the plate back to me, he looked very well. His cheeks were almost pink.

'I really enjoyed that. Thankyou so very much, my dear little neighbour.'

As I slipped his knife and fork into the dishwasher, I started to feel palpitations of anxiety. Suddenly, out of the blue, I was assailed by a host of mottoes: Children must not be spoiled, Rock a baby in your arms and it will never sleep in its cradle, Give an inch and they will take a mile. From that day forward, Monsieur Dupotier wasn't going to be satisfied with just stale biscuits and soggy crisps. He was going to be wanting couscous at every meal. He would come and claim his rights as soon as the smell of frying onions wafted under his door.

Well, you'll have to open up a soup kitchen then, won't you, dear. Well played. I was going to pay a high price for my peace of mind.

As is often the case, I was actually a far cry from the dramatic consequences my kind gesture would have.

The following morning there was a sign pinned to the old boy's door: PEOPLE IN THE BUILDING ARE FORBIDDEN TO FEED MR DUPOTIER. Those unsteady capitals, written in biro, betrayed a hand that didn't do a great deal of writing.

I stood on the doormat for several minutes, stupefied. I thought of the signs you see in zoos. FEEDING THE ANIMALS IS STRICTLY FORBIDDEN.

Moses and Nestor love wandering around the zoos at Vincennes and at the Jardin des Plantes. I love taking them there, not only because I like making them happy, but also because I have an almost metaphysical curiosity for animals, their smell and the way they move. I can never resist a trip to the zoo, and I'm quite an authority on them. The zoo in Regent's Park in London, or the one in the Bronx in New York, the one at La Palmyre near Saint-Palais, the Tête D'Or animal mini-park or the Pépinière Gardens near the place Stanislas in Nancy. I compare them, in an amicable way. The bears don't seem very happy in one place, but the pelicans are in their element. I know that some people think zoos are the saddest places in the universe; they might even go so far as to accuse enthusiasts like myself of sadistic voyeurism. They love it at the end of *Planet of the Apes*, when the men end up behind bars. Personally, I've always thought that scene was absurd and ridiculously dogmatic. Men behind bars? Yeah, right . . .

There are some wonderful true stories about zoos and their directors in times of crisis. There's the one that happened during the Second World War. Mr Saito, the director of Tokyo Zoo, was ordered to kill all the dangerous animals because the authorities were afraid that if the zoo were bombed, the lions, snakes, crocodiles and venomous spiders would escape into the streets. Mr Saito was supposed to make his way round the zoo with the appropriate syringes, guns and asphyxiating gases. But he really loved his animals. So he decided to put them up in his own home. His house wasn't very big, and his wife was terrified. The elephant couldn't get through the door. The pythons languished in the bathroom. I think he ended up being eaten by a tiger. I don't know what happened after that, I have a problem with stories: I forget them too quickly to tell them. I just like to imagine the house being hit by a bomb, and a lion slinking through the streets, frightening all the adults whereas the children would have been thrilled to see him running so fast and so free . . . before starting to worry about its safety, not their own.

I tore the piece of paper down, and went and knocked on

Simone's door, shaking slightly, frightened that I might be shot between the eyes.

'What exactly is this?' I ask her, holding out the crumpled piece of paper.

I see that Simono isn't in the *loge*, and I relax a little.

'Was it you who gave him some couscous?' she asks in a voice that's both whingey and furious.

'Absolutely. And, believe it or not, I'd give it to him again, because the poor old man's starving.'

'It's easy for you to say that because you didn't have to clear up afterwards,' Simone bellows. 'Your food only gave him diarrhoea. I've got better things to do than clean his sheets, I can tell you.'

I'm about to capitulate. I'm in the comfortable position of someone teaching someone else a lesson, while Simone's been landed with all the lowly tasks.

'That isn't the problem! No one's got the right to do this. If I want to give Monsieur Dupotier something to eat, you're not going to stop me.'

'But it's not my fault,' Simone snivels. 'His daughter-in-law told me to put the sign up. She doesn't want him to keep bothering you. She doesn't want people in the building complaining.'

'Who's complaining? Have I complained? It's my business. If I don't want my neighbour to die of starvation, I've got a right to feed him.'

'No.'

'What do you mean, no? I'm not going to let this stop me.'

And I tear up the piece of paper right under her nose.

'Don't do that, Sonia,' begs the *gardienne*. 'His daughter-in-law will have me. She's the one giving the orders.'

'No one's giving *me* any orders. Give me her phone number. I'm going to call her straight away.'

Simone scribbles the number on the scrap of paper I'm holding out to her. Then she looks at me, powerless. She daren't do what she really wants to do, which is to put me in my place. Her submission makes me feel uncomfortable. It's like a rather bad joke about class struggles.

I go home and shut the front door of my apartment, my heart weighed down with guilt. I think that if I'd given the old boy a nice little *blanquette de veau* there wouldn't have been such a fuss. It must be that Arab stuff that made him ill. It's because it was couscous that the daughter-in-law got a bee in her bonnet.

I think about Simone's hang-dog expression again, her subjection. I humiliated her. I talked to her with all the disdain of a rich cultivated young woman who can afford to refuse any sort of compromise.

Someone answers after just two rings.

'Madame Dupotier?'

'Speaking.'

'I'm your father-in-law's neighbour.'

'Oh.'

Her voice, her disgust, her loathing chill me. She could turn my blood to lead. I know instantly which tribe she belongs to. Why didn't I guess sooner? The heartless tribe, the tribe of hatred. I decide to play the 'nice girl next door who hasn't got a clue' routine, and to knock her dead with my good up-bringing.

'I'm so dreadfully sorry to disturb you, but I've just had a little altercation with the *gardienne* on the subject of Monsieur Dupotier.'

She doesn't say anything. She's inert. She probably reckons that anything she says will give me some purchase.

'It's an awkward situation, you see, because I found a little sign on his . . .'

'I asked for it to be put there,' she cuts in suddenly.

Her tone of voice informs me that she's the sort of woman who wouldn't have shied away from a public execution by guillotine.

'It must be very difficult for you . . .'

'You can say that again!'

Change of tactic. She's opted for aggression.

'I live a long way away. I work and I haven't got time to waste on this.'

I suppose that by *this* she means her father-in-law.

'I understand,' I say, about to give in. 'But, you see, I work too.'

What sort of idiotic jousting competition am I getting myself into?

'Get to the point, please. I've got better things than this to be doing.'

This time the *this* is me.

'I just wanted to say that these methods, I mean, how can I put this? I was really very shocked to see a sign like that in the building.'

'All I want is for him to stop bothering you,' she said more gently.

'He's not bothering us. He's hungry.'

'Listen, I give the *gardienne* enough money to feed him. There's no need for him to ask for people's charity.'

'I've torn up the sign.'

'What?'

'I've torn up Simone's sign saying we mustn't feed him. I think it was inhuman.'

'But how am I supposed to deal with this?'

'Why don't you ring Social Services?'

'I haven't got time.'

'I'll handle the whole thing. I'll go and queue up at the office. All you'll have to do is sign the forms. I'll find someone to look after him properly.'

'If it'll make you happy . . .'

She hangs up without another word.

I'm chewing my nails. I feel like crying, but I also feel like cracking the bitch's head open with a baseball bat, and pouring 90° proof alcohol into her nostrils. Hate is contagious, that's the problem. She's passed it on to me like a cold, and

I'm full of it now. Soon all these murderous urges of mine are going to land me in prison, and that reminds me of the last scene of *Planet of the Apes*.

After listening to *Für Elise* for forty-five minutes with the telephone under my chin, I get hold of the relevant department. I explain the facts to a woman who's very understanding but who, nevertheless, insists on asking me every few minutes: 'But who are you? A relation?' 'A neighbour,' I reply, 'just a neighbour.' This misunderstanding doesn't stop us opening a file and thinking about Monsieur Dupotier's future in a more optimistic light. Mme Corsotti, who promises me that she'll do everything she can to sort it out, is an angel.

I'm reduced to drawing lines on a piece of paper to calm my nerves. On one side there are the angels, led by Mme Corsotti, on the other the demons, headed up by the Dupotier widow. It's like being at the theatre. There they all are in their two neat rows and I find it very soothing distinguishing the goodies from the baddies.

Simono, the fat pig, on the right; Mr Lakrach, the butcher downstairs, on the left; the fascist lollipop-lady I had a row with last week, on the right; Jenny, at the nursery school, on the left.

Things get more complicated when Simone comes into contention. I don't know where to put her: whatever she does, she does it with disarming sincerity and a willingness to do what's right. I see her as a victim, and I wonder how

61

GOOD INTENTIONS

I would have fared as a prosecutor in a court of law. A great
champion of extenuating circumstances, that's what I am.
And what about me? I don't know where to put myself either.
On the left when I ring Social Services when the Dupotier
widow should be doing it; on the right when I exploit my
power over Simone to make her give in to me. On the left
when I give my neighbour couscous; on the right when I'm
ashamed of doing it; and on the right again when I admit
that I only did it so that I didn't have to throw it away. I'm
exhausted and appalled by these mental gymnastics. I've got
the moral awareness of a five-year-old. I carry on with it,
though, and all afternoon I look at that vertical horizon, the
dividing line by which I live and think.

I don't tell Julien about it. He's in a good mood. He's
driven the children to their grandparents, and he's asked me
to go out for a drink because it's one of those autumn
evenings you dream about, bathed in a red glow. The sunset
is making the leaves on the trees turn from green to gold,
and when they fall it's just the logical conclusion of this
chromatic sequence.

I didn't want to go to the Bar des Alouettes, but Julien's
persuaded me. The plastic tables on the terrace have spilt
over onto the pavement. We've ordered two pastis and
he's talking about Feng Shui again, explaining that it is
pronounced 'fung shoo-ay'. They're going to make some
openings on the East side of the building, he announces
proudly.

I wonder whether I shouldn't go straight up to Monsieur Dupotier's apartment to check which way it faces.

The sun daubs my lover's forehead with ochre. His eyes are shining and his shoulders seem to be getting wider. He's got that rare air of victory about him, that all-conquering smile that I so love to see on his face. When I look at him I forget about the day I've had, about my life, I forget myself and my endless questioning. I tell myself that if he weren't called Julien, he would be called *yes*, because it's one of my favourite words.

All around us people are chatting and sipping their drinks. There are old people trying to look younger, and young people trying to look older. I want to enjoy myself and to make the most of this moment of pleasure, but my thoughts keep straying. Confronted with my lack of enthusiasm, Julien's conversation steadily runs dry. Soon we're sitting in silence and the bustle around us is invading our table. I can feel the anger rising inside me, like a prickling at the tips of my fingers, a nagging ache at the back of my neck. I can't stop thinking about Monsieur Dupotier, and about his daughter-in-law who's waiting for him to die with monstrous intensity.

I tell Julien about the business with the sign. I know I shouldn't, but it's stronger than me. I give him a jumbled account of all the little details that made up the day; it's painfully boring and pointless.

Julien ironically sings the opening bars of a nostalgic ballad about dead partisans, gazing absently at the other side of the boulevard. I feel that we don't belong to this time and place. We don't even belong to this season. I've brought a burden of suffering onto our shoulders, and we can't do anything to shrug it off. The weight's coming alive and clinging to our shoulder blades, digging its claws into the thin flesh over our ribs. We each consider what we stand to lose. This is how it's going to be, we're condemned to seeing things in allegories, to thinking of everything as a reminder of previous atrocities. Simone's sign, the notices at the zoo, swastikas above shops, *Arbeit Macht Frei*, Please keep off the grass; from the most harmless to the most appalling, the most naive to the most cynical, all these words seem to have been written by the same hand. How can we break free?

I've ruined the evening. Now we're left in despondent gloom. I wonder whether this isn't a strategy of mine to avoid making love, and then I accuse myself of reading too much into things. The way the other customers in the bistro look around kills me. I can't see what they were looking at, how do they do that? I just can't bear the fact that not one of those dozens of pairs of eyes is shedding a single tear. I feel like getting up onto a chair and shouting, telling them all about the sign and Monsieur Dupotier, and, while I'm at it, all the other stories, feed them all evening on lists of tortures, stop them believing in Father Christmas, in God and peace, and their own disgusting self-satisfied comfort.

Julien eyes me harshly, he knows what I'm thinking. Dismayed at the prospect, he takes my hand and tells me I've got a terrible habit of behaving as if I'm Jesus Christ. I laugh, but I hate him. Who's going to have me if even he thinks I'm mad?

We sit stiffly, our chins set.

'You've got to stop doing this,' he challenges.

'Stop doing what?'

I know exactly what he means, but I just want him to say it.

'You can't think about anything else.'

He means that I'm wallowing in it, and that's what he's afraid of, but I want him to find the words.

'It's easy for you, you're never at home. But I'm stuck at my desk from morning till night doing these stupid translations. How do you expect me to ignore him? If I don't answer the door he only comes back ten minutes later. I've already tried.'

'Write poems.'

'What?'

'I said write poems.'

I suddenly feel like putting a sign round my neck saying: It is strictly forbidden to get inside my head.

'No one does that any more.'

'I'm not talking about wearing mini-skirts. I'm talking about writing poems.'

'You don't know anything about it. You're in your own world. You don't know what goes on in mine.'

'That's not true.'

'Jacques Prévert,' I say, very loudly.

'What about him?'

'You're not laughing. But it *is* a joke. Everyone laughs when you say Jacques Prévert. He's that thing that the teachers keep feeding to our children as if he was going to make them grow big and strong, but, apart from them, no one gives a stuff about him.'

'So what?'

'That's it. I've said my bit.'

'You're cheating. Anyway, I like Jacques Prévert.'

'I'm just saying no one does it any more. That's all. Apart from anything else, I'm a girl. And girl's poetry is pretty dodgy. Why are we talking about this?'

'Because I want to talk about something that isn't Monsieur Dupotier.'

I look down. It's true. It's all we talk about. That or the children. I feel ashamed for our love, our poor beleaguered love.

6

The Artists

What I really want is to go for a walk. The sky is a perfect ink-wash blue. Sitting in a chair with my back hard up against the radiator, I'm looking out at the long, black, leafless branches of the acacia. They look like spiders' legs, gracious agile forms caught scurrying through the air. But it's too cold. The chill turns our cheeks to steel and our fingers to wood. You only have to walk a hundred metres for your eyes to start streaming. You feel naked, cut to the quick.

Last night we didn't get home until two o'clock in the morning after a boring dinner party that we just couldn't leave. Right up to the last minute I kept hoping that one of the other guests might start talking normally, or laugh, or even just sniff. There were ten of us and everyone was vying for attention with depressing assiduity. All anyone could talk about was work and money. I couldn't see what the stakes were. Having withdrawn in the first half hour by asking for a glass of water while every one else was drinking vodka, I'd very quickly melted into the background.

As we left, I kissed Julien, as if we didn't know each other, as if we'd met for the first time at that terrible dinner party.

And it worked. I felt that little shiver somewhere around my navel.

Outside our building, Simone was slooshing great bucketfuls of water over the pavement. She was wearing just a flimsy lacy jumper and a knee-length skirt, with nothing between her bare feet and her ancient slippers, as she did in the middle of summer. The steam which came billowing up when the hot soapy liquid came into contact with the freezing tarmac formed an other-worldly cloud around her.

'What the hell's she doing?' said Julien.

'Can't you see,' I replied, 'she's doing her housework.'

Simone, who's incapable of running the vacuum cleaner over the stairs, was scouring the pavements at just before two in the morning.

'She must be completely plastered.'

Julien knows a thing or two about alcoholics – there are several in his family. I always forget that they exist at all; my trusty solution for seeing the world as a better place. I found this reassuring because I had an idea that drinking warmed you up. Simone was full of wine, whisky, calvados, all sorts of different anti-freezes that would protect her from pneumonia.

'How are the artists, then?' she threw at us.

And I thought, she must like us, after all.

'How about you, aren't you cold?' Julien asked her.

'You don't get cold when you're working. And Niniche has only had to go to hospital. She's got double cirrhosis.

It's made all her varicose veins go. And I get landed with all the work.'

Niniche, so that was her name. Simone and Simono had got themselves a slave who appeared just before Christmas. There was something familiar about her face so we hadn't really noticed her. She was a local. Someone who said hello to us, and we said hello back, and she gave our children incongruous nicknames like Rodiddy and Tockymoo. She was small, with a slightly hunched back, and she looked like one of the dwarves from Walt Disney's *Snow White*. No, she was more like two dwarves. Somewhere between Sneezy and Dopey. Her complexion was particularly repulsive, like liver pâté that was going off. She was a fan of the same astringent hair-dye as Simone, but she hadn't mastered the use of it to such subtle effect, so that her frazzled hair looked like the tufts on the end of an old, dry maize cob. Her drooping, yellowish eyes squinted under tired lids in a constant, vain struggle to focus. There was a mad glint in her eye, and she talked to Simono's dog in a despairing, weary voice as if he were her only child and the disappointment of her life.

For the last few weeks she'd been hanging around in the stairwell with an old bit of rag over her shoulder and a bottle of window-cleaner in the pocket of her housecoat. She gave a little rub here, and a little dab there. This spasmodic activity had no connection with the jobs she was meant to be doing, or with the dust – it was just a series of reflex actions that her body needed to fulfil. As she lifted her arm up to draw rainbows of grime on the walls, her mouth smiled weakly and her eyebrows, straining with the effort, looked like tiny pointed rooftops. Niniche did all the work, not that there was much to do, with Simone's rudimentary notions of hygiene.

'Poor Niniche,' said Julien simply.

The *gardienne* shrugged.

'Shouldn't've drunk so much.'

The house still smelt of lamb cutlets and potatoes *dauphinoise*. It was warm, and Amandine, the baby-sitter, had fallen asleep. Before going to bed, I went all round the apartment like a policeman on the beat, with my hands behind my back, walking with slightly martial authority. I saw the sheen on my children's foreheads like bulbs of mercury in the darkness. I listened to them breathing, and breathed in their smell. I thought about what Julien had told me. To write poems. Why not? But what would they be about? My sons' skin, the kisses I drop into the crook of their hands when they're asleep; Julien's hands, his slender neck, his dark impenetrable eyes that make him look wary, suspicious? I felt so mawkish and at the same time so inspired that I would willingly have banged my head against the wall. But I'm not an artist, whatever Simone might say; I don't have nervous breakdowns, my emotional landscape is a smooth plain.

Sitting in my chair, with my back against the radiator, I'm watching the spider-legged trees, waiting for a poem to land in my lap. I want to be concise, razor-sharp, but I'm too bowled over by the splendour of the sky for that. If it weren't so cold I would go out. I picture myself with enormous legs, the rooftops scarcely reaching my thighs. I could cross the city in just three strides, and up on the hills at Saint-Cloud I could lie down on the tops of the beeches, ashes, poplars and plane trees, a giant fakir, tickled by the rows of prickling branches.

Down in the street I can hear noises: the butcher's assistant in his white hat throwing quarters of beef and halves of lamb over his shoulder, the muffled roar of cars, dogs barking.

A drumming sound starts up somewhere. A very gentle ba-boom, ba-boom, as if the building's heart had suddenly started beating. A few seconds silence, and then it starts up again. The water pipes are arteries, the electric cables are veins, the lift shaft is a backbone, the corridors are lungs, the twisting staircase intestines, all those windows are eyes (some animals, molluscs I think, have as many as three hundred eyes). It's the only thing I can hear now. So my wish has been granted. The magic that I've been waiting for, on which I've concentrated since I was five-years-old, the miracle of transmutation is happening at last. Something inanimate is coming to life.

'Help!'

The drumming's getting louder and I recognise that voice – hauntingly sad like a musical saw. Monsieur Dupotier asking for help. He's hammering his fists on his door. I jump to my feet. Make this be just another bit of my dream. I can't cope with any sort of danger.

I go out onto the landing and ask, 'What's the matter? Don't be frightened. It's me.'

'Help me, my dear. Please help me.'

'What's happened. Come out. Have you hurt yourself?'

The neck of the femur, that's what it must be. The elderly have skeletons like little birds.

'I can't get out,' he says, still knocking against the door. 'They've shut me in.'

'Who has?'

'The caretakers. They've taken my key.'

He's got to calm down. I can just picture him on the other side. He's going to end up injuring his hands.

'Keep calm. I'm going to set you free.'

I think I must have nicked that phrase from Zorro or Robin Hood. But unfortunately, I'm not made of the same stuff as those dispensers of justice. In this particular instance, I'm short of a few burgling techniques. A winch, a jack, a crow-bar, a hairpin – I run through all the tools that could save the situation. The lock looks very complicated to me. Flooded with admiration for the petty criminals who laugh slyly about doors, even re-inforced ones, I opt for a method better suited to my lack of experience.

'Don't worry about a thing, I'm going to get the key from Simone.'

'You're so good to me, I was frightened here on my own.'

Simone, own, I think – as my poetic impulses surface at an inopportune moment.

I go down to the ground floor and hammer like a woman possessed. They'll set the dog on me, I tell myself, imagining the pain from the bite mingled with the disgusting smell that the terrified animal gives off. No sign of life in the *loge*. I hope there's been a mass suicide. The thought of their three bodies lying on the ground is a relief. No, not Simone. Not Niniche. Just the fat pig, bled dry. This is the daughter-in-law's work. She'll spend the rest of her life in solitary.

I'm really losing the plot now, and I remember that I didn't get to bed until three in the morning. I ring Julien. He's Zorro. He's Robin Hood. My hero. As I dial the number, I think that the poems a woman writes for the man she loves are the most laughable things in the world.

I manage not to cry. As a reward, he says he'll come straight away. I wouldn't be surprised if he pitched up in the apartment on a big black horse. Oh Tristan, oh Hamlet, my knight in shining armour!

When he comes through the door with his mop of hair all tousled, looking so thin inside his bulky jacket, I immediately feel protective towards his skin, his joints, his soft, soft belly. I hug him to me, and he pushes me away.

'They're here.'

'Who?' I say stupidly.

'Simone and Simono. They're playing Ludo in the *loge*.'

'Listen!'

Monsieur Dupotier's hammering on his door again. 'Help. Help me.'

73

Julien shakes his head.

'This is ridiculous,' he says.

I don't understand. We're about to save a life, and saving a life is like saving the world.

'Be careful.'

'What could possibly happen to me? I'm going to go and ask them for the key. They'll give it to me and I'll open the old man's door.'

I can see he's disappointed. He was all ready for an ambush, for sabotage, complete with dynamite.

From our landing, I listen blindly to the whole scene. The shouted exchanges interspersed with the mad dog's barking.

'Open up!'

'What does that boy want?'

'This *boy* wants Monsieur Dupotier's key, and you'd better make sure he gets it.'

'Leave it, Simone, I'll deal with this. Piss off you prat.'

'Give me the key.'

'I'm not giving you anything. Shut up and go home.'

'I'm not moving till I've got that key.'

'Come and fight for it, then.'

I hear the door being pushed or pulled.

'Look, I said bugger off.'

'Give me the key.'

'He wants to fight, Simone.'

'Get out of here, you wally. You couldn't even fight, any-way,' from Simone and then Simono's voice again:

'You're going to regret this.'

'Give me the key or I'll call the police.'

'Call the police, call your mother, call whoever you like.'

'Give me that key or I will call the police.'

Julien comes back up, taking the stairs four at a time, and runs over to the telephone. I can hear the caretakers yelling at each other downstairs. I cross my arms over my chest to stop myself shaking. Monsieur Dupotier's still hammering on his door.

This is the end, I think. The police. I want to tell Julien not to do it, not to bring them into our home. I'm frightened they'll find drugs or accuse us of beating our children. The children! I must go and pick them up from school. In a complete panic, I throw on a coat, a hat and a scarf. The caretakers mustn't recognise me. I'll run past the *loge* and, on the way back, I'll tell Moses and Nestor to keep quiet. I'll tell them some story about a wolf hiding in the lift. That'll keep their mouths buttoned.

We arrive home at the same time as the police, and Nestor cranes up to my ear to ask if they've come for the wolf. The boys are impressed by the silver braid on their hats and their red, white and blue badges; they point at the guns attached by a sort of telephone wire to their belts as the three of them, two men and a woman, leap athletically up the stairs ahead of us.

'Are they real ones?'

'Yes,' I whisper.

Moses doesn't believe me. He thinks I'm getting more and more absurd in my attempts to make their lives exciting. He's convinced I've paid a couple of actors to give some credibility to my lame story about the wolf.

'Anyway,' he says, 'wolves are nearly extinct. They've been hunted out, decimated.'

His younger brother looks at him dubiously.

'Perhaps this is the only one left,' he suggests.

Moses shrugs his shoulders, but his scepticism soon wavers. He moves over towards the sergeant, stretching his hand out towards his gun, and the man doesn't even look round as he says: 'Get the children out of here, please.'

I take them to their rooms and tell them to stay calm.

'Are they going to kill the wolf?' Nestor asks.

'Be quiet,' says his brother.

Then, turning towards me, he asks: 'If you and daddy go to prison, could we go and live with granny?'

'Moses, you're completely mad,' I tell him. 'The police are here because Monsieur Dupotier's lost his key. He's shut in.'

My son looks at me, disappointed.

I leave them in their room, closing their door to all the lies.

Why is it so difficult to tell the truth? Once you start lying, you can never stop. And yet I feel as if my wolf story is closer to the facts, more faithful to the situation than an objective report of the events. My syntax is running on empty. As usual, I'm finding it impossible to describe only what I see and hear, and nothing else; it just doesn't seem enough.

Julien once told me about an artistic movement, I don't remember what it was called, whose only principal was to stop painting; I laughed till I cried.

'You mean there's a whole load of painters who've decided not to paint?'

'That's right.'

'Well, what do they do then?'

'All sorts of things. Some of them have jobs in factories.'

'Are you taking the piss?'

I laughed so much . . . and it hurt him so much. Now, though, I feel like building a little pagan shrine to them. Now I – the one who can never stop talking, the chatterbox who's always got something to say about everything – I feel like abstaining from speech. The words that I've been given, that I've inherited, are no use. The world is a tissue of metaphors and you can't tell anything straight.

We've given our statement. Our neighbour, Monsieur Dupotier, has been illegally confined to his apartment by the caretakers of the building.

'Hey, now! Illegally? Watch what you're saying,' says the sergeant.

He smiles at his acolytes as if sharing a joke with them at my expense.

'They've taken the key,' I say to be more specific.

The three police officers sigh wearily; they've seen plenty of cases like this. This isn't a sufficiently spectacular problem for them. They're bored. There's no blood, no severed limbs cut into pieces. It occurs to me that, like us – but for precisely the opposite reasons – they're disappointed by their mission.

They're the same age as me, we could have been in the same class at school. The one in charge is quite red in the face with narrow shoulders and wide hips; he reminds me of Pascal Trénaux, a boy who was in the second year with me and who didn't give a damn about anything until a misplaced word would suddenly set him off. The blood would come rushing to his face, transforming him on the spot. His whole body would quiver with electric impulses, he would throw punches, leap in the air, scream, lash out at people and throw himself on the ground. We would watch him, speechless and mildly amused, but a little bit afraid as well. 'He must have suffered a lot when he was little,' the school nurse had confided in me, but I didn't believe her. I'd already made up my mind that suffering was not an excuse.

His stooge is shorter, squatter, with no neck, so that his head emerges from his shoulders like an egg from an egg-cup. He has a voice like a bugle with a slight southern accent. He stands with his thumbs tucked under his belt watching us, Julien and myself, mockingly. He thinks we're a waste of space, that Julien's weak and effeminate and that I'm ... well, just a woman.

The woman with them is nothing like me, it's true. Her blond hair is drawn back into a tight pony tail and she has the tilted, jutting chin of a stubborn child. I'm particularly impressed by her strong build; she has big, red, powerful hands. She's standing perfectly still, with her feet slightly apart, ready to draw her gun, or to pin any passing bastard to the ground to get him in an arm-lock.

A lock, precisely the problem.

'Right then, if I've got this right,' the sergeant recaps, 'your neighbour can't get out of the house, and you're worried about it.'

'I haven't got your details,' cuts in the girl, suspiciously.

We meekly rattle off our full names, address and marital status.

'Profession?' she asks, smiling in anticipation of our answers.

'Architect.'

'Translator.'

She winks at the two men.

'Artists, then!'

They start laughing and then, almost regretfully, their expressions say: well, that's not all there is to it, we're going to have to let this poor old boy out.

Five minutes later we hear Monsieur Dupotier's door being opened. He throws himself into his saviours' arms, can't think how to thank them. Julien and I go out onto the landing. He kisses our hands. The police officers look away and, without a word, head off to check a few brake-lights – well, they have to find some way of justifying their stroll along the boulevard.

I drop down onto the sofa, exhausted. I haven't shed a tear, but my eyes still feel wrung clean.

'They thought we were a couple of idiots,' Julien says.

But then we hear footsteps on the stairs. It's Simono coming to settle the score with the old man. I close my eyes. I want him to stop existing, to trip on a stair, to turn to water, to implode.

'I'm coming to bring him his grub,' he says to Julien who's shot out onto the landing.

'If you touch a hair on his head . . .'

'Don't try and be clever with me, you prick. One day – you won't know how it's happened, but I'll know why – you'll find yourself out cold on the street. With a bullet in your head. I won't miss.'

7

The Baddies

Monsieur Dupotier has come to see me. It's the third time this morning.

Here I am back at the beginning of my story. Another ten months have passed and Christmas is nearly upon us; a fertile season for nervous breakdowns and despair. The dark sky over the streets is peppered with white bulbs depicting stars and sleighs.

I think about the story of the Christmas orange, the most highly prized present given to a poor boy. When I was at school the teachers used to bang on about him so much you'd have thought he was a saint. He kept it carefully under glass and ... we never really knew what happened next, I suppose he watched it rot. An edifying fable if ever there was one, intended to bring tears to our eyes and to stop us clamouring for expensive electrical toys from our hard-pushed parents.

We ignored Christmas in my family because it was a Catholic celebration. The birth of Jesus was no big deal. We held our heads high in the face of all those dazzling shop windows. We thought it was cruel to fell all those pine trees who'd never asked anything of anyone, and we felt a mixture of contempt and envy for the stampede of lunatics hurling themselves on the silver garlands and scarlet baubles.

The children who believed in Father Christmas, in presents coming down the chimney, in reindeer launching themselves into the snowflaked sky, seemed exaggeratedly naive to us. Meanwhile, in order to stand our ground, we had to invent even more fantastic beliefs for ourselves. Perhaps these idiotic fantasies that still burgeon in my brain stem from that, from this forced agnosticism. It's one of my greatest assets, the fact that I have the right to believe in whatever comes into my head. The trees talk, the stones listen, the sky is thronging with strange creatures. No one has the right to tell me it's not true because I've learned to see reality in a different light. I do still sometimes feel that I'm a bit of a misfit. When I feel like that, I'm prepared to go to great lengths to get back onto the right tracks.

Once when I had a free morning I decided, in the hope of curing myself, to make a list of things that don't exist but in which I believe, then a list of things which exist but in which I don't believe. The result was frightening. In the column *Things which exist but in which I don't believe* there was, for example, *sex*. Well played, I told myself. Now there's a wife and mother coming to terms with her situation. I rang Bianca, an Italian friend who was older, wiser and more experienced than me. She'd had a hundred and fourteen lovers. When I asked her, she didn't seem surprised, she said 'Hang on, I'm just getting a cigarette'. Anyone else would have asked me to repeat the question. I wouldn't have dared, I would have laughed to make them think it was a joke, thereby missing a unique opportunity to find out about the world, the real one, the one I don't understand at all. But Bianca likes questions. She has a taste for polemics, which is the twin brother of a taste for love.

'Yes, it does exist,' she confirmed, 'but mostly for men.'

'Why mostly for men?'

'Partly because of castration anxiety . . .'

Bianca's pretty well up on psychology, as am I, but it's like sex, in the sense that I don't believe in it.

'. . . and also for the simple reason that they're made to think about it all the time.'

I liked the idea of 'made to think about it' – so much more imperious and, therefore, more *risqué* than just 'reminded of it'.

'They're frightened they won't be able to get it up,' she explained.

'Yes, yes, probably. It must be very worrying,' I said without any real compassion.

'And also, you've got to realise that, when they see a pretty girl, the subject . . . comes up. They know that they think she's pretty before they've even realised she is.'

'What about us?'

'What *about* us?' asked Bianca.

'Does it do that to us too?'

Bianca laughed. 'It does in a way. But what's the

matter, are you having problems with Julien or something?'

'No, it's just for my list,' I told her, and she had the immeasurable goodness to accept that as an answer.

I hung up, I went to look at myself in the mirror. I wondered whether I was pretty. I imagined boys' members rising as I walked past, like a guard of honour. Impossible. Bianca talks a lot of rubbish. It doesn't exist.

As I grew up, I managed to cancel Christmas, to think of this time of year as just a huge promotional fair. I think of the compulsory transhumance that most of my friends undertake as they visit their parents and find themselves, especially if they don't have children of their own to spoil, in the uncomfortable position of overgrown babies who are supposed to coo with delight as they open a series of disappointing parcels. I also think of the elderly, like Monsieur Dupotier, who no longer have anyone to make a fuss of, and don't even have the alibi of wrapping and delivering presents to take their mind off the cold nights closing in by mid-afternoon.

Simone and Simono have hung a silver wreath over the door to the *loge*. It says *Happy Christmas*. Who's this message addressed to? To the people who live in the building, to Niniche who's finally come out of hospital and is mopping the floor? Niniche who's ended up turning into a floor mop – her hair's like the lank threads of old cloth and her big yellowy eyes are like the bubbles of detergent on the surface of a bucket of dirty water. I realise that she isn't only the caretakers' slave, she's also a metaphor for their decline, the physical incarnation of their debauched existence, a pure concentrate of their corruption.

Simone and Simono never change. I've known them for seven years now. I've acquired a few wrinkles and I've watched my children grow; a supermarket has opened; a Chinese restaurant has closed; various bars have come to give new life to the blind façades blackened by smoke; someone's business premises caught fire; the town hall changed hands; there's now a huge advertising hoarding in the little square – about as incongruous as a bird table in the middle of the Sahara; some houses have been knocked down; others have been built, glass and tile creations which look like giant igloos and make you feel cold just looking at them; tall young men in woolly hats roller-skate sinuously along the streets with messenger bags slung across their chests. Simone and Simono have stayed the same. No new note of weariness shows in their dark-ringed eyes, no bitterness has traced telling furrows round their dry lips. Niniche has got the lot instead. Like a major blow to the head. She even dyes her eyelashes now. I think it must sting your eyes when you do that. With these prickly white hairs along her eyelids she looks more and more like those deep-sea creatures that are half-fish, half-lizard, born blind, eking out a slimey existence in the icy depths of undiscovered caves. She has difficulty speaking, her mouth has lost the necessary muscle tone to articulate. She shrieks and grumbles and utters some senile drivel, her arthritic fingers clutching the walking stick that she never lets out of her grasp, although she forgets to use it when she walks.

What does he want now, I ask myself as I leave my computer. Monsieur Dupotier's already had a croissant, half a baguette, the breakfast that Simone brought up for him and some biscuits.

'Hello, my dear.'

'Hello, Monsieur Dupotier.'

'What's the time?'

I look at my watch, as if the exact minute matters to him. But Monsieur Dupotier's no longer in our time scale. He's going backwards while we go forwards. To him the seconds seem to draw out into infinity, and the days run into each other. The sand in his hourglass trickles away one minute, then runs the other way up for no reason, then stops flowing altogether.

'Quarter past six.'

'I'd like some oysters.'

'Sorry?'

'I'd really like some oysters.'

All that makes me think of is Simono's dirty green eyes, of his gobs on the pavement.

'I haven't got any,' I say, disgusted.

'But I really would like to eat some oysters.'

'What do you want me to do about it, Monsieur Dupotier? There are loads of things I'd like to eat too, and I make do with what's in the cupboard. Okay? So, come on, you go home now. It'll be supper time soon. Simone'll bring something up for you.'

I shut the door on him even though he didn't show the least sign of withdrawing.

That was down to the Christmas effect. Why not some caviar while he was at it? In my day, we used to make do with an orange, that's what I should have told him. I'm going to cook some potatoes for the children who are playing very nicely in their room with toy soldiers. I can hear their voices – made especially virile for the occasion – making oddly anodyne exchanges. My two ventriloquists aren't in bellicose vein this evening:

'Are you a friend of Batman Pirate of the Seas?'

'No, I'm the Galactic Defender of the Frozen Continents, I'm the friend of Batman Fatal Shield.'

'Could you ask Batman Steel Armour if he wants to come to my birthday party?'

'He said yes, but he wants Batman Rocket-Thrower and Batman Atomic Bazooka to be invited too.'

'Tell them we're having the best Nutella sandwiches.'

'I prefer honey sandwiches.'

Obviously, this culinary conflict doesn't necessitate an immediate attack. The little plastic figures advance on their rigid little legs, shake hands stiffly and sit in a circle round a table of Lego. Balls of plasticine represent a feast which would make Monsieur Dupotier blanch with envy.

I think about our digestive system, of all that food we have to swallow to give us ... muscles in the case of spinach, brains in the case of fish, or good eyesight if carrots are on the menu. I tell my children all sorts of stories to persuade them to eat their food. There are the usual ones: soup makes you grow, meat makes you strong; but there are some that are more home-spun: courgettes, for example, aren't really courgettes but *cretacettes*, vegetables that lay forgotten for tens of thousands of years, in fact the only vegetables that dinosaurs used to like eating. Sometimes I wonder why I go to so much trouble, and exactly what sort of joy I feel when – miracle of miracles – they finish their food without my abusing their naivety.

The children have eaten well – it's incredible how good it is to hear that and what a pleasure it is to say. There's a saying, isn't there, 'you are what you eat'. I could even have invented it, and purists will have to forgive me this because, personally, I couldn't live without it now. 'You are what you eat,' hence the desire to give our children all that is good and lovely to eat. 'You are what you eat' and, conversely, you eat what you are.

That's when I wonder why Monsieur Dupotier's suddenly got an urge to eat oysters. Christmas. He wants to eat what everyone else is eating to create the illusion that he's partici-pating. I know he won't have any turkey or Christmas cake, and I want to persuade him that he can survive without either.

'What's going on now?'

I didn't hear the door, and Julien makes me jump as he comes into the kitchen. He's swaddled in a scarf, and gesticulating expansively towards the sitting room with his strangler's hands cramped into a pair of leather gloves.

'Nothing, everything's fine,' I say.

'Haven't you seen the ladder?'

'What ladder?'

'Outside.'

I look at him with owlish eyes. I don't know what he's talking about.

'Simone's taking the old man's food up on a ladder.'

Julien leads me into the sitting room and opens the window. The *gardienne*'s disappeared, but the ladder's still there, on the pavement, leaning against Monsieur Dupotier's balcony.

Julien goes downstairs to find out what this new development means. When he comes back up he explains that our neighbour's lost his keys.

'But he was here just ten minutes ago,' I say incredulously.

'Where here?'

Julien's annoyed. I don't know who he's annoyed with, but as I'm the only person here at the moment, I take the rap.

'On the landing. He asked me for some oysters.'

'Oysters?'

'Because it's Christmas.'

I went past the old people's home on the way home. It has a big bay window overlooking the road to the boys' school. Like a giant cinema screen on which virtually nothing happens. In the dining-room old people sit round tables on ordinary chairs and wheel-chairs; their heads seem strangely detached from their bodies, stretching forwards, like vultures' heads. Their faces are pale. Their skin is like faded poppy petals. Their hands, gripping the arm rests or curled up one inside the other, look as if they're asleep. Their eyes gaze aimlessly, heavy as stones, murky as troubled water. Some sit with their jaws hanging open, others have their lips tightly sealed, clamped over each other as if they're being sucked from the inside. You feel like shaking them, picking up the whole dining-room and shaking it like one of those transparent aquatic globes inhabited by minute elves, dancers or clowns, so that synthetic snowflakes float down onto their heads. There are strings of coloured lights along the ceiling and down the pillars, flashing in time to Vivaldi's *Four Seasons*, barely audible through the window. Garlands of silver letters flitter in the up-draught from the convector heaters. Not one of the inmates moves. The nurses talk to them, stroke their fragile heads, and put things in front of them: pictures, packs of cards, multi-coloured sweets. Their tea looks oddly like the one put out for the cohort of Batmans in my children's bedroom.

I often console myself with the thought that Monsieur Dupotier's better off in his own home, that he can still talk and remember, that the pain afforded him by his memory is worth the having, it's certainly better than the miles of white sheets parading silently through the mindless heads of the old people in the home.

On my way home from the market the following morning, I see Simono putting back up the ladder that he tidied away in the cellar the night before.

'Haven't you got another set?'

He jumps at the sound of my voice and then turns towards me slowly. He runs a hand through his slicked back hair, and sighs. A woman's just spoken to him and he looks as bemused as if his dog had started serenading him. He gives me a long, slow, contemptuous stare, with his chin tilted towards me and his jowls drooping.

'You just can't help sticking your noses into everything, you lot, can you?'

I want to ask him who he means – women, people my age? But I suddenly realise what the answer is, and it sends a chill through me. But we've got a perfectly ordinary French name, what better mask could we have? I must have confided in Simone, back in the days when I still thought of her as a guardian angel, a fallen one granted, but well-meaning all the same. Simono must have heard my father speaking a few words of Arabic with the butcher downstairs. He's asked a few questions in the area. He did say he'd been in the police force, didn't he?

'You didn't give me an answer. I asked you whether you had another set of keys?'

'Oh really?' he said loftily. 'I didn't hear anything. I'm a little hard of hearing. I go deaf just watching you going up the stairs in your floaty little skirts.'

He's pleased with himself now. And I'm ashamed of myself. Ashamed of the thoughts he's dressing me up in, ashamed that he can take my body, if he so pleases, and make me act out all sorts of disgusting games in his perverted dreams. How could I make him feel like that? Nothing will ever hurt him. I think about David and Goliath, but there's no sign of a sling anywhere. I tell myself that no torture could ever go beyond his ignominy because everything about him is already corrupt. He'd only cry in pain, not with regret, not with sorrow or despair. There isn't a person inside him, he's a nothing, and I leap to the philosophical conclusion – in which I believe even less than I believe in Father Christmas – that that in itself is his punishment. There isn't a person inside you, I tell him without speaking.

'Now what's that face for, little girly? Come and tell daddy whassa matter. Is it the old man's key?'

'Yes,' I reply weakly. 'I'd like to know what you're planning to do.'

'Ring the locksmith and send the bill to the daughter-in-law, sweetheart. It's as simple as that.'

'I warn you, you're going to have to sort it out very soon.'

'Well, would you look at her on her high horse. Look,

you're not the one that the widow's paying. It's got nothing to do with you. D'you understand? Now it's my turn to warn you: don't go getting ideas about pissing us around like last time. The old bill've got better things to do than listening to daddy's girls like you simpering.'

I know he's lying, but I haven't got any ammunition to make him admit it. They've shut him in again. Monsieur Dupotier must have said something to them about oysters and they've decided he deserves to be punished. I can't imagine where they get this endless supply of cruelty.

As I go up the stairs, I can hear him still hammering on the door. 'Help,' he says in that irritating voice of his. I catch myself thinking: Shut up, you stupid old man. Why can't you die, just die, for pity's sake.

'I'm here, Monsieur Dupotier,' I say from the landing.

'My dear little neighbour! I've lost my key again. I'm going mad in here.'

'Don't worry. They're going to call the locksmith. Keep calm. Simone's going to bring your food up.'

I leave him to snivel so that I can go and watch the operation from my window. As I predicted, the *gardienne*'s on the ladder with a bowl of coffee in her hand. She's got the bread and butter in her apron pockets. She curses as she climbs each rung because the coffee keeps spilling and burning her fingers. Bloody pissing buggering shit, stupid bloody old pain in the arse, Christ this sodding bastard coffee, why can't the stupid old bugger die. I lean over to watch, my hands freezing as they come into contact with the balcony rail. Simone's only wearing a cardigan over her slip, her bare calves are going blue. But she doesn't resent the cold, because she's too busy resenting the old man. If you offered her a knife, she'd willingly slit his throat. But she keeps thinking about the thirteen hundred francs that the daughter-in-law gives her every month. Thirteen hundred francs – the price that dreadful woman has put on her father-in-law's survival.

When I rang her to find out what stage the formalities had got to with social services and the local council, she told me that everything had been cancelled, because it would have cost her two hundred francs more than she was paying at the moment.

'I can't afford to throw money out of the window, you know.'

No, I didn't know. She didn't have any children, she no longer had a husband, she had a job and she stood to inherit a sizeable sum of money.

'All the same, it would be better,' I suggested. 'He'd have help round the house. His flat is really very dirty, you know.'

'It's disgusting, you mean. He's completely let himself go. I'm ashamed of him. Poor Simone has got better things to do.'

'Exactly,' I ventured. 'If the local council intervened, it would be a great relief to Simone.'

'Well then you can pay the extra two hundred francs if you want to waste good money.'

'If that's the only problem, then I will, gladly.'

She said nothing for a moment, stunned by my reply. She would have been less surprised to see a Martian stepping out of her fridge.

'That's impossible,' she said eventually in a tart voice. 'You're not family.'

It was on that day that I told Julien I never wanted to speak to the woman again. 'If we have to call her back, you'll have to do it.' He agreed to it. She didn't frighten him, she was only a human being, a species for which he seemed rather better prepared than myself.

'It's just two hundred francs, can you believe it?' I wailed. 'She'll get the money back in less than a year at the rate things are going.'

'There's no guarantee of that. Monsieur Dupotier is in good nick underneath it all. If he were properly fed he might well last quite a long time.'

'Is it murder then?' I said, horrified.

Julien shook his head and smiled. He felt sorry for me and my astonishment.

'What do you think?'

The baddies, that's what I think. The baddies are joining forces.

Simone knocks on the old man's window, and he opens it to take his breakfast.

'You haven't found my key by any chance?'

'I've said it's lost, haven't I?' she yelps at him as she climbs back down.

I'm still watching her. She doesn't look up at me. She mutters insults and gives the ladder a good kick when she reaches the ground. I wonder what she's getting out of all this. It can't be much fun doing acrobatics in your slippers in the freezing cold.

That's when my mind goes off at a tangent. I smile to myself and think what reality would be like if I were in charge of it. If I invented what was real, Simone would take Monsieur Dupotier's meals up with the tray balanced on the top of her head, so that both her hands were free to grip the rungs of the ladder. With each step she would recite verses about the glories of nature, sunlight on the morning dew and dog roses opening in the soft light of dawn. I've got a head full of what Simono would call simpering.

It starts snowing in great thick flakes. Suddenly there's snow everywhere. Snow doesn't just fall from the skies like rain; it could just as easily be coming up out of the ground, floating and swirling, appearing from nowhere so that you wonder how you didn't notice all these white dots just moments before. Simone's still out on the pavement, she looks up, opens her mouth and flutters her eyelids, offering her flat face to the icy, feathery flakes. Then she sees me.

'Isn't the snow beautiful,' she says.

There are snowflakes falling onto her cleavage, melting instantly.

'Get in, you're going to catch cold,' I tell her.

She looks pretty like that, seen from above, round and stable, with her hands on her hips like a spinning top.

The snow's coming in through the window. I'd like it to come down from the ceiling too. In just a few hours everything would be clean and white and sparkling. I'm very confused. It's snowing in my head too. I'm deadened, blunted by the cold. I tell myself I've invented the whole thing. Monsieur Dupotier, his wicked daughter-in-law, the wicked caretakers, the threats, the blows, the deprivation; none of it exists. The only thing that's really here is the snow, the snow and the silence it creates.

But the ladder's still there.

In the evening, we ring the police. My stomach ties itself in knots at the thought of it. What will they find to hold against us this time? I think about my overdraft, the unpaid fines, the road tax we haven't bought, our faces, our clothes. Clean the whole apartment. Feed the children early. Act normal. But we don't have any choice. Julien went down for one final negotiation, which achieved nothing. Or rather it did – it produced an unbelievable explosion of anger, the flood gates opened and the torrent of insults flowed freely.

'I'm not gonna open his door, you prick. It's you I want to slit open. I'm gonna smash your head in and splatter it all over the walls.'

I stood on the landing, listening. The children came to see

what the noise was, and I told them to go back to their room. I wondered whether I should intervene, and I felt weak and cowardly. Julien wasn't saying anything. I tried to imagine him, my precious dark-eyed saviour, my fearless featherweight. Simono could easily have launched himself at him with his revolver.

I went down the stairs on tip-toe, worried by a sudden silence in the stairwell. They stood facing each other outside the *loge*, the good and the ugly, the brave and the despicable. Julien was tapping the floor gently with one foot, beating out the time to some mysterious song in his head. Simono glared at him defiantly, his huge belly and his flabby, drooping breasts thrust forward like the prow of a ship. Saliva hung in little strings from his bared teeth. He was ready to bite.

'Are you a Jew, then?'

Julien didn't reply.

'Do you know what they do to Jews where I come from?'

Julien stayed absolutely motionless.

Simono curled one of his thumbs back and ran it across his throat as if it were a knife.

'We do 'em in.'

Julien nodded two or three times and then turned away without a word. Very slowly, he climbed the stairs towards me. I felt like telling him to run, to jump, to vanish from the caretaker's line of fire as quickly as possible. I was frightened he might take a bullet between the shoulder blades, or have a knife hurled at his back. I held him in my arms and burst into tears.

'What's the matter now?' he asked, exasperated.

'It's horrible. Didn't you hear what he said? Didn't you see what he did?'

'So what? It's not really front page news, is it. You didn't think he was a great fan of Freud and Kafka, did you?'

'They're still the same. Just like in 1940.'

'Why do you expect things to change? It's not going to do anyone any good if you keep bringing all that up. I'm going to call the police.'

My immediate thought is that we mustn't refer to the racist insults, because in 1940 the police were in on the whole thing and, given that nothing changes . . .

'Good evening, ladies and gentleman.'

There are three of them, like the last time, two men and a woman.

She turns to me and I try as best I can to explain the situation to her. She takes notes and opens her eyes wider and wider with each detail I give her.

'This is like something out of *Les Misérables*, I haven't just seen the play, me, I've read the book, you know!' she exclaims in response to my shaky explanations.

Right now I could prostrate myself at her feet. She understands, she thinks it's disgusting, she's read Victor Hugo.

The officer takes Julien's statement, while the third

policeman tries to persuade the children that there are far more exciting things going on in their bedroom.

Julien doesn't omit a single detail, I watch him miming Simono's throat-slitting gesture, while the officer shakes his head.

'Stupid sod!' he says.

I can almost hear that music you get when the cavalry arrives in a cowboy film. I think they usually had grey tunics, but of course there are the blue tunics too.

'And you haven't tried to get into your neighbour's apartment?'

'No,' replies Julien.

'Perfect. If you had, that would have been breaking and entering. That would have made things much more complicated. Right, wait for me here, I'm going to let the gentleman out, and we'll take care of the other two while we're at it.'

The officer opens the window and steps nimbly over the balcony. After taking a few careful steps along the ledge, he knocks on Monsieur Dupotier's window.

'It's dangerous,' I say.

'The boss is a good man,' replies his deputy.

I ask the young woman what they're planning to do.

'We're going to take Monsieur Dupotier to hospital for observation. Have they beaten him?'

'Not recently,' I say.

'He'll go to hospital for a while, anyway. That's the correct procedure.'

'And what about the caretakers?'

'We'll stick 'em in prison,' says the boy with a shrug.

He's younger than us. His *képi* is too big for him, and his uniform hangs off his adolescent frame.

'What a mess,' he adds.

Now, that one didn't find his vocation in life watching Punch and Judy, and cheering Punch on with every blow; he must have spent long Saturday afternoons in front of the TV, admiring Serpico, Ironside and Kojak. He told himself that a bit more justice in the world would be no bad thing, and that he might be able to make a contribution himself.

I'd like to offer them a cup of tea or coffee, but I'm worried they'll say: 'Not when we're on duty.'

Order is a powerful force – there, that's what it is. Law and order have finally come into our lives and everything's going to go back to the way it was before. I can stop worrying that the mad dog's going to eat my children, or that Julien's going to take a bullet between the eyes. I'll be free to come and go as if nothing's happened. I'll no longer look for signs of life behind the dirty lace curtains in the *loge*, or worry that the children are making too much noise when they come home from school. I won't have to warn friends who come to see us that the caretakers are mad and might be dangerous.

It's only by enumerating these things that I see just what a reign of terror that fat pig's succeeded in establishing. I realise that for several years I've held my breath whenever I go up the stairs, with my heart hammering and my stomach churning, and suddenly it all strikes me as absurd. How could I have been so frightened? Why did I put up with it? That fat pig managed to revive all my childhood fears.

I know that Simone didn't really have much to do with it. But there's the whole question of whether or not she was in collusion with him which doesn't seem very clear to me. I'm weak and so easily influenced that I can't help feeling sympathetic towards the *gardienne*. Everything that Simone did, she did – according to my version of events – out of love for this brother, or rather lover. Out of fear, too, because more than once I saw the same expression in her eyes as in the mad dog's eyes. He was probably beating her too. Maybe he threatened her with his gun. Simone and Simono were particularly good at domestic scenes. They out-screamed the TV. I never managed to unravel the subjects of their rows, but they were terrifyingly violent. It was never long before the dog was yelping and being kicked in the ribs, or smacked over the nose with a slipper.

A dictator seized power on the ground floor of our building, and we did nothing to stop him. It went on for three years, as long as Nestor has been alive.

He wasn't happy just torturing Monsieur Dupotier, he wanted to rule over everything. The exact spot where Madame Calmann's dog was allowed to lift its leg, what time the girls on the third floor had to be home in the evening; he turned the place which had always been reserved for bicycles into a special parking space for his side-car, and he convinced us all that he'd been promoted to the position of caretaker for the underground car park of the modern building next door. It's true that for a few weeks he wore a grey uniform with an orange band on the sleeve which said 'security'. He directed the traffic from the central reservation on the boulevard, and he gesticulated helpfully to young women, who hadn't asked him for anything, when they were reversing into parking spaces, sniggering 'women drivers!' to himself. If he'd had the financial means, he would have put a security strip under the doorway to know exactly who was coming and going, and when. He walked all over us, and we let him.

I can hear Simone crying downstairs while they put the handcuffs on her, she's struggling and hurling insults at the policemen. It's not fair, I tell myself, because I know that Simone's got a heart. Is that an excuse? What wouldn't I do out of love? Except that I would never fall in love with such a bastard. There, I've found the fatal flaw. The consequences may have been understandable, but the choice was unacceptable in the first place. Let's ignore the love element, and just look at the fear. If someone beat me and threatened to hurt the people I love, how far would I go to placate them? I don't know why, but I just can't imagine myself in this situation, because I've been lucky in life, I've been looked after, I've never wanted for anything. The poor little rich girl's back on the scene. Could this whole thing just be to do with class? No, I'm getting side-tracked because it's probably just that blood is thicker than water after all. Let's say Simono *is* Simone's brother; she can't help agreeing with him because they grew up together, because they started tearing the wings off butterflies together when they were very young.

The policemen asked us to sign some papers, and I watched out of the window as the two vans with their flashing lights moved off along the boulevard. In the ambulance: Monsieur Dupotier. I didn't even have a chance to say goodbye to him. In the police van: the caretakers, Simone in tears and Simono issuing all sorts of death threats. Everything is very quiet now.

Moses comes out of his room to ask us what's been going on.

'The police have taken the caretakers away,' his father explains. 'And a doctor's going to take care of Monsieur Dupotier.'

'Has he gone too?' asks Moses.

'Yes.'

'When's he coming back?'

We can't answer.

'I'm going to ring the daughter-in-law,' Julien announces.

I admire his courage, and go to take refuge in the children's bedroom.

'That woman's unbelievable,' he says after he's rung up. 'I think she gets first prize in the nastiness stakes.'

'I hope you congratulated her.'

'Oh, warmly, yes. When I told her that the caretakers had locked the old man in again, and that they'd been taken away by the police, all she could find to say was "what a pain!"'

'What does she mean, what a pain?'

'"And who's going to look after my father-in-law now?"' Julien imitated the widow's shrill voice. 'Your father-in-law doesn't need anyone, he's in hospital, under observation. "And when he comes back, who's going to look after him then?" The place is full of people looking for work, it won't be difficult finding someone. "But how am I to know if they can be trusted?" Oh, I see, you thought that Simone and that fat brother of hers could be trusted, did you? People who beat up an old man, threaten him, starve him and lock him up in his own home, you think they can be trusted?'

'What did she say to that?'

'Nothing. She just said "what a pain!" again.'

'Stupid bitch!'

We decide to open a bottle of champagne. But we don't have one, so we get drunk on vodka.

Julien is slightly the worse for wear when he receives a telephone call from the CID: he's got to go and make another statement straight away.

'What if they breathalyse you?' I say, pulling at the sleeve of his jacket.

'The plaintiff has got every right to drink. The plaintiff can do whatever he likes.'

'Don't forget to take some form of ID.'

It just so happens that Julien has had a number of unfortunate experiences in police stations.

'I'm going to the CID, my sweetheart. The CID is like *Inspector Morse*, serious, big boys' stuff, *comprendes*?'

Julien gives me a series of rather incompetent winks and I think to myself that he's certainly more cheerful when he's had something to drink. I picture a comfortable, alcoholic retirement, and I close the door behind him, crossing my fingers so that he doesn't come to any harm.

8

The Statement

In the morning, Paris is white. We all ought to take this opportunity to hibernate, but humans aren't that sensible. On my way back from the school, I bump into Niniche in the lobby. She smiles at me and asks for news of the boys in her incomprehensible gabble.

Should I apologise to her? Or should she actually be thanking me? We have, after all, sent her oppressors to prison – at least that's what I believe at the moment.

She's free, she's got nothing to do, she doesn't recognise herself. A martyred skivvy suddenly raised to the rank of Captain, feeling her way with bemused caution. She's still very jumpy. She hears voices, she remembers the sound of a hand rushing through the air to slap her, she spasmodically brings her hand up over her head to protect herself from the blows . . . but she's smiling once more. She asks me to help her sort the mail because she can't really work it out.

She daren't tell me she can't read, and I manage to find a way of avoiding mistakes: I make a little bundle for each floor and number them; she won't have any trouble with numbers. Unfortunately, the whole exercise becomes rather more complicated when she has to distinguish between left and right.

'Leave it, Niniche, I'll do it,' I say.

'Oh no, you mustn't. It wouldn't be right.'

From her tone of voice, you'd think I was the queen mother.

'I don't mind. Really. I can take the lift.'

'Well, I'll come with you then.'

Why's she being so polite, as if making amends? She wants to show that she respects me. It's odd, but I don't let this soften me. Niniche was made to obey, she's chosen me as her new master. I'm appalled by this promotion, and I resent her for not seeing that I'm not like Simone, or Simono.

The ride up in the lift is terrible. Niniche keeps touching my arm to get my attention so that she can tell me stories that I don't understand because she articulates so badly. She talks in erratic fits and starts. You never know when she's finished a sentence. She tugs at my sleeve, chuckles and goes completely silent. Then starts again. I look at her drooping cheeks, her sagging little forehead, a strange colour and texture which remind me of blocks of halva sweating under cellophane.

We start our rounds on the sixth floor. Each time I bend over to slip the envelopes under the doormat, she imitates me, bending over with me and breathing heavily as her stomach is constricted. On the fourth floor we meet Madame Calmann heading off to the market. She looks at us, Niniche and me, and then tilts her head at me with a questioning expression. Too overwhelmingly lazy to bother doing anything else, I just greet her politely, as if nothing strange is going on. This is my new life, my calm expression informs her: from now on, I do everything with Niniche; she's my shadow, my right arm you might say.

When we get back down to the ground floor, I feel the performance has gone on long enough.

'Bye, bye, Niniche. I'm going up to work.'

'When are they comin' back?' she asks mournfully.

'Never,' I say pitilessly.

'Isn't Simone comin' back?'

'No.'

'And Monsieur Pierre, isn't he comin' back neither?'

'No.'

'Where are they, then?'

Niniche was there, mind you, the previous evening when the police took the caretakers away.

'They're in prison.'

'What've they done wrong?'

I decide not to answer. I have as much chance of being understood by a dog as by her. I tell her she should go and rest, because it's the best thing to do and because I'm worried that, otherwise, she'll stay rooted to this spot all day. Niniche has that kind of inertia peculiar to orphans. Shuffling slowly on her short, ulcered legs, she makes her way over to the chair, and slumps into it, simultaneously pressing on the TV remote control. I myself shut the door to the *loge* to protect myself from the jubilant prattle of a game-show host.

*   *   *

What is it with today? I feel as if I've come home from a funeral, empty, floating. I find it impossible to work. I envy Julien who'll be forcibly distracted by the people he's working with and whose mind will be compelled to apply itself to solving problems. I peer at my dark grey computer screen irritably, resenting it because it doesn't give me anything or ask me for anything. I wish I could cut the spool of memories playing through my head, I wish something or someone could stop the incessant hammering of people's names, because just hearing them makes me unhappy. Simone, Simono, Monsieur Dupotier, I won't ever see you again. You're out of my life. I've thrown you out. I've won. But I don't want this victory. Come back. You mustn't disappear. The responsibility's killing me. Just let me give you one good smack. Not you, Monsieur Dupotier. I'll feed you, I'll give you proper meals, good food full of vitamins.

I'll give Simone a little slap on the wrist, and Simono a good kick in the stomach, perhaps also a swipe with a club on the bridge of his nose and in the teeth. Then I'll feel better. We'd all calm down and we could start again like before.

Nothing makes sense to me any more. I'm sitting on the carpet in the sitting-room and I feel as if I'm suffocating. My brain can't use logic just as a fish out of water can't use the oxygen in the air. How did I end up in all this? Who decided to throw Simone in my path? What's going to happen to Niniche now? Where's Monsieur Dupotier gone? Who's going to punish his daughter-in-law? Why didn't the other people in the building do anything?

When Julien comes home, he finds me sitting on the floor, hugging my knees. I haven't moved for hours, I haven't eaten anything, I'm rocking languidly, daydreaming. He's got bags under his eyes, his eyelids are purple, his jaw tense, he looks like an accident victim.

'In the Inspector's office . . . No, he wasn't an Inspector, just the policeman on duty. A pathetic bloke. You wouldn't believe the conditions this bloke has to work in. His office is a tiny little room painted khaki right up to the peeling ceiling. There's nothing in it. Just a table and two chairs. No posters on the walls, no telephone, a bare light bulb and a second-rate radiator. On the table there was a typewriter that must have dated back to when the place was built. At least two of the keys weren't working and, each time he had to use them, he banged on them five or six times. 'o-o-otherwise, i-i-it d-d-d-doesn't mark the c-c-carbon paper,' he said.

'Do you remember carbon paper? The last time I saw it I was in the fourth year. He was very nice. A great long face with lots of red hair and a goatee beard. He stammered so badly that I tried not to give him a chance to speak. Each time he had to say something, he held his breath as if he was about to dive underwater which didn't help because he was exhausted by the time he got to the second word, you see.

'At first I didn't think I should talk for him, so as not to upset him, but I soon realised that he didn't mind, that it actually suited him fine. Everything I found out about him in the space of two hours came out of my own mouth.

'It was me who said that he'd been living alone with his daughter since his wife died, that you never fully recover from the death of a loved one, that life is appallingly cruel and the most difficult thing of all is the terrible silence at meal times. It was also me who explained that once he reached his retirement the only thing left for him would be to throw himself in front of a métro train.

'Our little problem, I mean the problem with Monsieur Dupotier and the caretakers, was all dealt with in five minutes. It only took half a page. It seemed a bit skimpy to me, but when I read it through I didn't have anything to add. Since the table was crooked and he could only keep it steady by balancing it with his knees, most of the words had a few letters amputated. In places there were three s's in a row or two commas. But as far as the meaning was concerned, it gave the essentials. *On two occasions, at an interval of one year, Mme Chiendent and M. Lacluze, caretakers of the building, locked M. Dupotier, owner of a first-floor apartment, into his apartment.* "It's not such a big deal really," I told the policeman. But he disagreed. I spoke for him, I said: "On the other hand, they could have killed him. It was an abuse of power over someone who was dependent on them. They also beat him and intimidated him." The policeman nodded as I said this. While we were talking, two reports were dropped on the table by some weirdo with bulging eyes who laughed as he talked. "Two real bastards, ha, ha, ha." "These are real, first-class low-lifes, hee hee hee." The policeman read them out to me with great difficulty. Simone's already made a couple of court appearances for – what did they call it? – pimping, basically, and Simono for aggravated whatever it's called and for attempted assault.'

'What does aggravated mean? Aggravated by what?'

'I don't know. I didn't ask.'

'And does attempted assault mean murder. Has he tried to kill someone?'

'It must do, yes.'

I shudder retrospectively, thinking about the silvery gun.

'So are they going to go to prison?'

As if asking whether the princess gets married at the end of the story.

'I don't think so.'

'Why not?'

'The policeman was pretty embarrassed; he led me to understand that they couldn't do much to them.'

'So what does that mean?'

'It means that Simono is probably an informer, he's probably protected by someone higher up.'

I would never have found the solution to this enigma on

my own, because in my mind Good and Evil always have to be clearly separated by a ditch, a river, some insurmountable barrier.

If one of the baddies makes himself useful, he doesn't get punished. It's a sort of trade that you can't ignore.

I have to accept this untidy fact, I have to understand that it's no longer a question of cops and robbers. 'Which ones are the baddies?' I used to ask as a child when I was watching television. The answer came quickly. 'The baddies are the ones wearing hats.' 'The baddies are the cowboys.' 'The baddies are the Germans.' 'Why are they baddies?' My parents preferred this second question. They told me about battles for land, about economic crises, and I came away in a state of exhausted confusion; not only did I no longer understand a single thing about the film, but I was also thinking: it's not their fault if they're baddies, and if it's not their fault then they aren't really baddies. So who *are* the baddies? Because it seemed to me that, despite the rational explanations I was fed to reassure me, there was something dark and unfathomable about the world, a terrifying, insidious, destructive force. I would huddle in my bed, eyes closed, teeth clenched, petrified. My heart would beat faster and faster, I thought I would die. Everything became jumbled in my mind: lava from volcanoes, venom from spiders, people who stole children, and those who killed them, soldiers who tortured people, bottomless pits you could never climb out of, avalanches, car crashes, trains trundling people to concentration camps, solitary confinement cells, atomic bombs. With all that, I really couldn't see how I was going to cope.

I'd like to tell you a story about a turtle. I saw it on TV swimming in a turquoise lagoon. I learned from the commentary that she was called Lili. She was adorable, as only a turtle can be, flying rather than swimming, with a doddery head that had the beguilingly childish ability to dive for cover under the shell, only to pop out again like a jack-in-the-box. Lili was the heroine of the programme, and you obviously didn't want anything unpleasant to happen to her. You didn't want the sun to be too hot for her, and you wanted the sea to provide her with plenty to eat so that she'd be strong enough to continue her journey. All of which duly happened, the meal arriving in the form of a squid which didn't have a name and could, therefore, be eaten without causing too much distress. She started with its head as it swam backwards, and it was a while before it stopped moving, she bit first into one eye and then the other. When she was about to swallow its tentacles, a shark appeared. It didn't occur to me that there could be any form of danger in this encounter. The shark was quite small and I had faith in Lili's instincts: she would duck safely into her little shell and sink to the sea bed like a stone. I can only think that the pleasure of her feast must have prevailed over her caution because she carried on eating, giving the predator time to speed over to her and grab her head which he tore off with one gnash of his teeth. I sat speechless in front of the television as the credits rolled over a background of green water tinged with scarlet blood.

9

The End

Forty-eight hours later the caretakers came home. The snow was beginning to melt. Footprints were appearing on the pavements as dirty grey and brown outlines, fusing together in every direction. The little snowdrifts round the trees were stained yellow where dogs had lifted their legs, and black where car exhausts had spewed over them. A layer of crystal-line sludge stuck to your shoes. It was damp. The sky was colourless, hopeless, reflected as blades of silver in the over-flowing gutters. Everything was collapsing around me, I thought, or was it just the thaw?

I rang Monsieur Moldo of the 'uni' to explain that we might have to take some sort of action. It didn't tally up. We'd got rid of Monsieur Dupotier, but the caretakers had come back. Well played.

'What's going on?'

'What's going on is that the caretakers are here, they've threatened my husband, I'm frightened, and I want them to go.'

'I can't do anything about it. They haven't committed a crime. They'd go to their industrial tribunal and they'd win, the co-owners' association just couldn't afford it.'

'So, as far as you're concerned, locking an old man in his home, threatening people's lives and calling them dirty Jews isn't a crime?'

'Not according to the labour regulations.'

'Give me an example, then. Tell me what would justify a dismissal.'

'Not emptying the dustbins. Refusing to distribute the mail, things like that.'

The new blood is going back to where it came from, my dear Monsieur Moldo. I thought that when the time comes for the next co-owners' meeting, if we stay in the building long enough to attend it, I might stop off at the eye bank on the way. Mine have seen too much. It might be a good idea to change them.

Monsieur Dupotier never came back.

Three months later, we moved.